BRITAIN & THE EUROPEAN UNION

BRITAIN&
THE EUROPEAN
UNION

Simon Adams and Simon Ponsford

W
FRANKLIN WATTS
LONDON•SYDNEY

Franklin Watts
First published in Great Britain in 2016 by
The Watts Publishing Group

ISBN 978 1 4451 5062 8

Editor: Julia Bird
Designer: Mo Choy Design

Picture credits: AFP/Getty Images: 14. andriano.cz/Shutterstock: 12t. AP/Topfoto: 12b. areporter/Shutterstock: 21. Fabrizio Bensch/Reuters/Corbis: 38. Peter Bernik/Shutterstock: 31. Olga Besnard/Shutterstock: 32. Franck Boston/Shutterstock: front cover t, 3. Matt Cardy/Getty Images: 45. Memhet Cetin/Shutterstock: 40. Aidan Crawley/Alamy: 37. Drop of Light/Shutterstock: 20, 24. Nicolas Economou/Shutterstock: 43t. Peter Fuchs/Shutterstock: 26. handhiki/Shutterstock: 35b. Botond Horvath/Shutterstock: 22. Hulton Archive/Getty Images: 27. Hulton-Deutsch/Corbis: 10, 17. Dennis Jacobsen/Shutterstock: 33. Julinsky/Shutterstock: 34bc. Aija Lehtonen/Shutterstock: 15. Media Guru/Shutterstock: 43b. Christian Mueller/Shutterstock: 29. Maks Norodenko/Shutterstock: 35t. JL Ortin/Shutterstock: 19. PA/Topfoto: 18. Johan Paborn/Alamy: 34t. Photosebia/Shutterstock: 28. Rex Shutterstock: 6, 23, 41. Slavko Sereda/Shutterstock: 36. symbiot/Shutterstock: front cover b. Takashi Images/Shutterstock: 34b. US National Archives/wikimedia commons: 16. Ververidis Vasili/Shutterstock: 25. viada93/Shutterstock: 42. Vojtechvik/Shutterstock: 7. cc wikimedia commons: 11. Xinhua/Alamy: 44. Bahadir Yeniceri/Shutterstock: 34br.

Every attempt has been made to clear copyright. Should there be any inadvertent omission please apply to the publisher for rectification.

Printed in China

Franklin Watts
An imprint of
Hachette Children's Group
Part of The Watts Publishing Group
Carmelite House
50 Victoria Embankment
London EC4Y 0DZ

An Hachette UK Company
www.hachette.co.uk

www.franklinwatts.co.uk

MIX
Paper from
responsible sources
FSC® C104740

CONTENTS

WHAT'S IT ALL ABOUT?

More than half a billion people today live in the European Union (commonly called the EU), making it the world's third-largest population after China (1.3 billion) and India (1.25 billion). Twenty-eight countries in total are members of the EU. France has the biggest land area, Germany has the most people and Malta is the smallest on both counts. The EU's borders stretch from the freezing cold of the Arctic north to the intense heat of the Mediterranean south, from the Atlantic to the Aegean.

An EU festival brings together young people from many countries.

WHAT IS IT FOR?

The EU was set up in the years immediately after the Second World War (1939–1945). France and Germany had gone to war with each other three times in seventy years, and now pledged to work together in peace and friendship. Six countries joined the Union at first, a number that has now risen to 28, with another six European countries waiting to join. The greatest achievement of the Union is to have kept the peace in Europe for more than sixty years, as none of its members have ever fought each other. The Union has largely abolished the old frontiers that used to divide the continent and has brought its member countries together through common economic, social and environmental policies.

JOINING THE CLUB

EU members include a unique mix of people, languages, cultures and traditions, who live in a community that wants peace, freedom, prosperity and social justice for everyone. Every European country can apply for EU membership, but not all want to join. It is a club where the rules are always changing, and people have very different ideas about what the Union is and how it should be run. Diversity can be the EU's strength. But it can also be its biggest challenge, especially now that 28 nations are competing to get their own voice heard. Each country is trying to juggle their national interests with those of Europe as a whole.

THE POWER OF THE UNION

The EU is not a federation like the United States, but neither is it only a gathering of countries like the United Nations. In other words, it is not a state that replaces the ones we already have, but it does go further than just international co-operation. Member states agree to hand over power to the EU on issues where they believe they will have more success and strength working together. However, the EU only has the powers that member countries have chosen to give it. For example, pollution takes no notice of borders, so EU members have agreed common rules that everyone must follow. At least half of all national laws begin life as EU laws. Individual countries still have the right to choose what to do about issues, such as defence or foreign policy, but they often act together to pack a bigger punch. For instance, there are now EU peacekeepers in Bosnia-Herzegovina.

★ The EU flag: 12 stars in a circle, symbolising the ideals of completeness and unity.

STRIKING A DEAL

The EU's work is based on agreements called treaties. To put them into action, three main institutions have been created: the European Parliament, the European Commission and the Council of the European Union. You can find out more about how they work in coming chapters. Almost every deal is the result of a compromise between the national interests of all the countries in the EU, and those of the three institutions. Finding friends and allies, rather than confrontation, is how you get things done in the club of 28.

SUPERSIZE EU

When ten new members joined the EU in May 2004, it changed the face of Europe. At a stroke, the EU's surface area increased by one-quarter, its population by one-fifth. In population terms, it became the world's biggest single market. And after years of conflict and division, most of Europe was uniting again in a peaceful way.

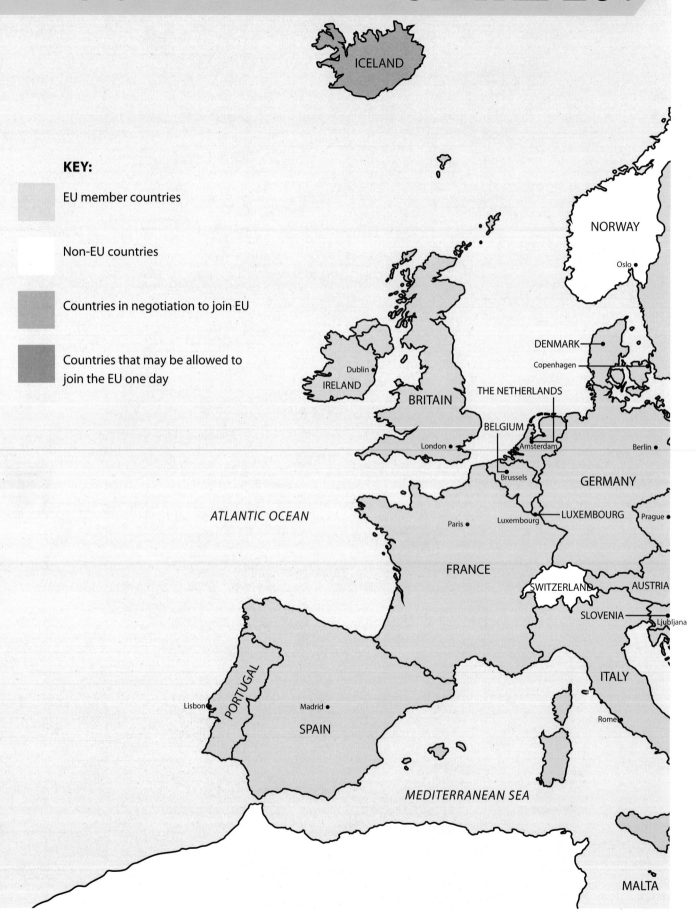

KEY:

EU member countries

Non-EU countries

Countries in negotiation to join EU

Countries that may be allowed to join the EU one day

ICELAND

NORWAY

Oslo

DENMARK

Copenhagen

THE NETHERLANDS

Dublin

IRELAND

BRITAIN

BELGIUM

Amsterdam

Berlin

London

GERMANY

Brussels

ATLANTIC OCEAN

Paris

Luxembourg

LUXEMBOURG

Prague

FRANCE

SWITZERLAND

AUSTRIA

SLOVENIA

Ljubljana

PORTUGAL

ITALY

Lisbon

Madrid

Rome

SPAIN

MEDITERRANEAN SEA

MALTA

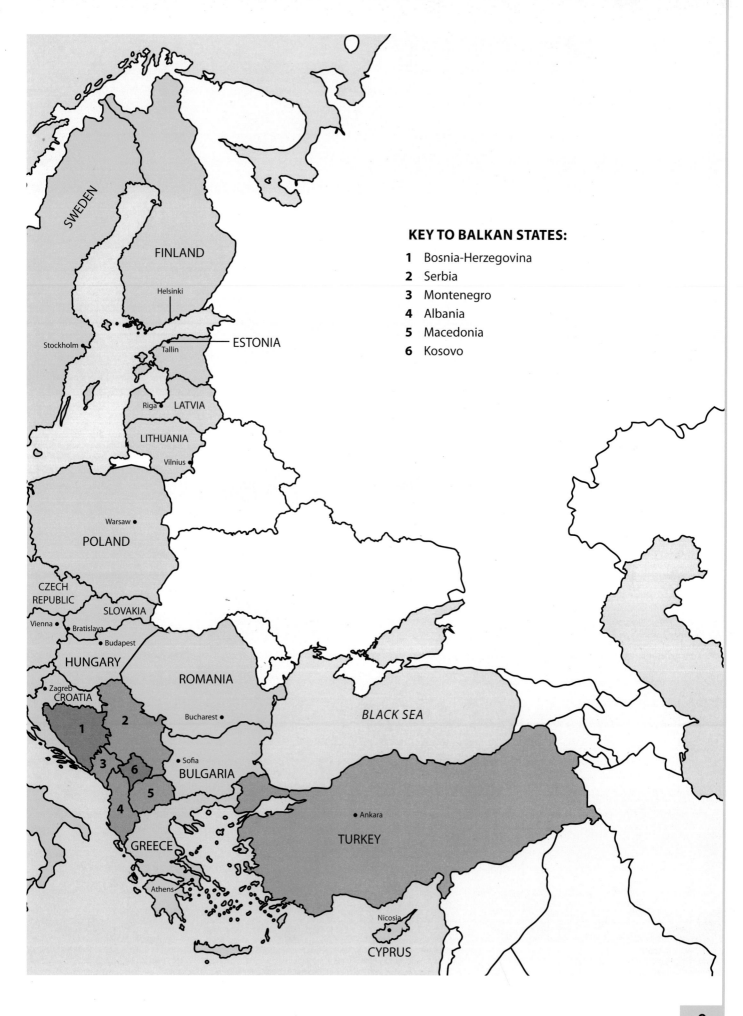

KEY TO BALKAN STATES:

1 Bosnia-Herzegovina
2 Serbia
3 Montenegro
4 Albania
5 Macedonia
6 Kosovo

SWEDEN

FINLAND

Helsinki

Stockholm

Tallin

ESTONIA

Riga

LATVIA

LITHUANIA

Vilnius

Warsaw

POLAND

CZECH
REPUBLIC

SLOVAKIA

Vienna

Bratislava

Budapest

HUNGARY

Zagreb

CROATIA

ROMANIA

Bucharest

BLACK SEA

1

2

Sofia

3

6

BULGARIA

5

4

Ankara

GREECE

TURKEY

Athens

Nicosia

CYPRUS

THE HISTORY OF THE EU:
PART ONE

The vision of a united Europe rose out of the killing and devastation of two world wars. People were looking for ways of making sure that Europeans would never again be locked in conflict with each other. They dreamed of the end of rivalry and hatred, and the beginning of a new era of peace.

★ Dresden, Germany, in 1945. Out of the ashes of war, European nations had to build again.

A MAN WITH A VISION

In 1946, Britain's war-time prime minister, Winston Churchill, summed up Europe's challenge:

'Over wide areas a vast quivering mass of tormented, hungry, care-worn and bewildered human beings gape at the ruins of their cities and homes, and scan the dark horizons for the approach of some new peril, tyranny or terror.'

His solution was 'to re-create the European family, or as much of it as we can, and provide it with a structure under which it can dwell in peace, in safety and in freedom. We must build a kind of United States of Europe.' Seventy years later, the building work still goes on, but Churchill's vision still rings true, with peace, safety and freedom at the heart of the EU project.

> **" We are not bringing together states, we are uniting people "**
>
> Jean Monnet, 1952

⭐ Jean Monnet (1888-1979), the architect of the European Union.

TIMELINE

1950 Driven by their dream of peace and prosperity for Europe, the EU's founders act. As a former assistant secretary general of the League of Nations, Cognac salesman and banker, Jean Monnet knows how to strike deals. He comes up with a plan for Germany and France to pool their production of coal and steel (the two main ingredients for making guns). The French foreign minister Robert Schuman takes up Monnet's proposal, and announces it on 9 May (the EU's birthday). He says it will make war between Germany and France 'not merely unthinkable, but materially impossible', and invites other nations to join.

1951 The Treaty of Paris establishes the European Coal and Steel Community. Belgium, the Netherlands, Luxembourg and Italy also sign up.

1957 The same six nations agree the Treaty of Rome. They set up the European Economic Community (EEC), aimed at boosting trade through the free movement of workers, goods, services and money. This will be at the heart of the European adventure. Members also create the European Atomic Energy Authority (Euratom), to aid the peaceful development of nuclear power.

1961 The EEC is a success. Britain, Denmark and Ireland apply to join, but the French President Charles de Gaulle is not impressed, accusing Britain of being too pro-US in its foreign and economic policy: 'Britain neither thinks nor acts like a continental nation, and so is not yet qualified for membership.' He twice vetoes Britain's application (1963 and 1967). Denmark and Ireland are also rejected, as they are considered too dependent on Britain to enter the EEC without it.

1967 The Merger Treaty creates a single set of institutions for the European Coal and Steel Community (ECSC), the European Economic Community (EEC) and Euratom, known as the European Communities.

1973 Britain, Denmark and Ireland are finally allowed to join after de Gaulle is replaced as president of France. Norway is also offered a place but Norwegian voters reject it.

1979 The Community plants the seeds of the single currency, the euro, with the introduction of the European Monetary System and a currency unit, the ECU. For the first time, members of the European Parliament are democratically elected.

1981 Greece becomes the 10th member of the EU.

1985 The President of the European Commission, Jacques Delors, paves the way for a 'single market'. It aims to take away all barriers to free trade or free movement of money or workers. The deadline is 1992. His plan comes after a long period of economic downturn, and fierce debate on what the European project is for, and how to pay for it.

(continues page 13)

THE HISTORY OF THE EU:
PART TWO

In the 1990s, as East and West Germany reunified and the Soviet Union collapsed, European leaders made plans for changing the face of their continent. There was a new name: the European Community became the European Union. There would be new rights for citizens, new economic freedoms, a new currency, a plan to expand eastwards and an attempt to rewrite the rulebook.

BUILDING FOR THE FUTURE

At the core of these changes was a deal signed by EU leaders in 1991, in the modest Dutch town of Maastricht. The famous Maastricht Treaty brought together the EU's three founding treaties. It ushered in a detailed plan for 'Economic and Monetary Union' (EMU), which would lead to countries all using the same currency, the euro. In Maastricht, heads of state agreed to work more closely together in areas such as the environment, education, workers' rights, health and safety and research. The EU became more political: it would take joint action on foreign and security matters (the new Common Foreign and Security Policy). There would also be improved co-operation in areas of justice and policing (the Justice and Home Affairs Policy), and countries agreed to work together on issues like asylum, immigration, crime, terrorism, drug trafficking and fraud.

★ Maastricht paved the way for the new euro currency.

★ European leaders sign the Maastricht Treaty in 1991.

TIMELINE

1985   Schengen Agreement to create open borders without passport controls between member states is agreed in outline by five EU member states.

1986   Portugal and Spain join EU.

1986   European flag is first used.

1986   Single European Act is signed, coming into force in 1987. It commits member countries to a timetable for single currency and common domestic and foreign policies.

1990   East Germany unites with West Germany and joins the EEC.

1991   Heads of state sign up to the Maastricht Treaty.

1992/93   European citizens vote in referendums on Maastricht, and many give it a rough ride. In France, it passes only by a 2% margin. In Denmark, voters only approve it the second time round.

1993   The Maastricht Treaty comes into force, renaming the European Economic Community (EEC) the European Community (EC). The treaty also sets up the European Union (EU). Under the treaty, citizens of the EU gain European Union citizenship. This citizenship is in addition to their own national citizenship and gives them the right to vote in European Parliament elections and the right to free movement, residence and employment across the Union.

1993   The newly defined Copenhagen criteria define the rules under which new countries can apply to join the European Union: all new members must be stable democracies, uphold human rights and the rule of law, and have a working market economy.

1995   Austria, Finland and Sweden join the EU. People in Norway once more reject membership. Under the Schengen Agreement, France, Germany, Belgium, the Netherlands, Luxembourg, Portugal and Spain end border controls between their nations. Other members (apart from Britain and Ireland) later follow suit.

1997   EU leaders sign the Amsterdam Treaty. One of its main goals is to prepare for enlargement: welcoming a big group of new members into the club. It also makes changes to the way that member states vote, and strengthens laws on issues like employment and discrimination.

1998   The EU begins membership talks with Cyprus, the Czech Republic, Estonia, Hungary, Poland and Slovenia. A year later, it is the turn of Bulgaria, Latvia, Lithuania, Malta, Romania and Slovakia.

2000   The Nice Treaty is agreed. It sets out the rules for an enlarged European Union of 27 members. It also lets groups of countries go ahead faster with some forms of co-operation, for example on defence. In the same year, in Portugal, the EU announces its 'Lisbon Strategy': plans for 'the most competitive and dynamic knowledge-based economy in the world'.

2002   Out go familiar national currencies like the deutschmark and the franc, in comes the euro. On 1 January, euro notes and coins become the official currency for 12 European nations. Sweden, Denmark and Britain strike a deal so that they will not join now, but might join later.

2003   The EU promises the countries of the Balkans that they too will one day become members.

2004   Ten new members join the club on 1 May: eight from the former communist bloc (the Czech Republic, Slovakia, Hungary, Poland, Slovenia, Estonia, Latvia and Lithuania) and two islands in the Mediterranean (Cyprus and Malta). In October, EU leaders sign a new constitution: a set of rules crafted to make the EU easier to understand, and to replace all the existing treaties.

(continues page 15)

> **❝** *From war we have created peace. From hatred we have created respect. From division we have created union. From dictatorship and oppression we have created vibrant and sturdy democracies. From poverty we have created prosperity. Our European Union is truly unique.* **❞**

From the declaration on Accession Day, Dublin, Ireland, 1 May 2004

THE HISTORY OF THE EU:
PART THREE

As the EU moves through its seventh decade of existence, it continues to expand and evolve. New members queue up to join, while existing institutions are revised and updated to cope with the many new challenges the Union faces.

LOWS AND HIGHS

The introduction of the euro has presented the EU with one of its biggest hurdles (see p.31), while a massive influx of refugees that began in 2015 (see p.42–43) has led to the reinstatement of border controls across much of Europe. Yet in many other respects the Union has proved to be a great success, bringing peace, friendship and increased prosperity to what was not too long ago a warring continent.

⭐ European commissioners and parliamentarians celebrate winning the Nobel Peace Prize in 2012.

> **❝** *Over a seventy-year period, Germany and France had fought three wars. Today war between Germany and France is unthinkable. This shows how, through well-aimed efforts and by building up mutual confidence, historical enemies can become close partners.* **❞**

Nobel Peace Prize Awarding Committee, 12 October 2012

WHO'S NOT IN?

Not every European country is a member of the EU. Switzerland is traditionally neutral and does not usually join international organisations, while Norway has twice narrowly voted against joining the Union. Iceland applied to join but then froze its application. However, Norway, Iceland and tiny Liechtenstein are all members of the European Economic Area, which provides for free movement of their people, goods and services within the EU, while Switzerland has a similar arrangement. The four microstates of Andorra, Monaco, San Marino and the Vatican City are all closely linked to the EU and use the euro. In former Yugoslavia, Macedonia, Montenegro and Serbia have all applied to join the Union, while Bosnia-Herzegovina and Kosovo are recognised as potential candidates. Albania and Turkey, most of which is in Asia, have also applied to join. To the east of the Union, Russia, Belarus, Ukraine and Moldova all remain outside the Union.

⭐ A poster celebrates Croatia joining the EU as its 28th member in 2013.

TIMELINE

2007   Bulgaria and Romania join the EU.

2007   The Lisbon Treaty is signed, coming into force in 2009. The treaty reforms many aspects of the EU, merging the three pillars of the EU – the European Community, Police and Judicial Cooperation in Criminal Matters, and the Common Foreign Policy and Security Policy – into one legal entity. The treaty creates the new post of President of the European Council and strengthens the role of the High Representative of the Union for Foreign Affairs and Security Policy. The treaty also recognises the existence of the European Council, comprising all the heads of government. In addition, the treaty agrees to move from unanimous to qualified majority voting in at least 45 key policy areas, and for the first time gives member states the legal right to leave the EU.

2009   Iceland applies for membership of the EU but puts its negotiations on hold in 2013.

2010   International financial crisis forces the European Central Bank to bail out the economies of Cyprus, Greece, Ireland, Portugal and Spain, all members of the euro.

2012   The EU receives the Nobel Peace Prize for having 'contributed to the advancement of peace and reconciliation, democracy and human rights in Europe.'

2013   Croatia joins the EU as its 28th member.

2015   Lithuania joins the euro, making it the 19th member.

2015   More than one million refugees from mainly Afghanistan, Iraq and Syria cross by boat into southern Europe. The influx causes considerable social and economic tensions across the EU.

2016   Britain successfully negotiates changes to its conditions of membership of the EU. In a referendum to decide whether Britain should remain in the EU, the British electorate voted to leave.

BRITAIN ON THE OUTSIDE

We have already read Winston Churchill's stirring call in 1946 to 're-create the European family' and build 'a kind of United States of Europe.' But what Churchill had in mind was not the European Union we have today, but a permanent council or meeting of European states to work together to keep the peace and promote human rights and democracy. This difference of view marked Britain's relationship with the rest of Europe for decades.

> **66** *We have our own dream and our own task. We are with Europe, but not of it. We are linked but not combined. We are interested and associated but not absorbed.* **99**
>
> –Winston Churchill

KEEPING OUT

After the war ended in 1945, France and West Germany began to work closely together to put aside their troubled history. Britain, however, was more concerned with the future of its worldwide empire and was not interested in any form of European unity. Britain thus stayed out of the negotiations that led to the Treaty of Paris in 1951 and crucially stayed out of the negotiations that led to the Treaty of Rome in 1957 and the founding of the European Economic Community. Gradually, however, the mood in Britain began to change. The Empire was slowly breaking up, while the special relationship

★ Allied leaders meet in Casablanca in January 1943. Discussions between General de Gaulle of France (third from left) and the other leaders were often tense.

GOING IN

Britain enjoyed with the USA no longer brought any economic benefits. In 1960 Britain helped to set up a rival trading organisation with six other nations known as the European Free Trade Association (EFTA). Although this was a success, it was clear that the EEC was the best organisation to join. In 1962 the Conservative government of Harold Macmillan applied to join the EEC. After a year, the French government of General Charles de Gaulle vetoed Britain's application, as he did not believe that Britain was pro-European enough. De Gaulle also vetoed a second application in 1967 by the Labour government of Harold Wilson.

After de Gaulle resigned as French president in 1969, and was replaced by Georges Pompidou, the veto on Britain's application to join the EEC was lifted. Negotiations began in 1970 under the Conservative government of Edward Heath. The negotiations were successful and on 1 June 1973, Britain joined the EEC. However, not everyone was happy with this change of direction. Many people in the Labour Party did not like the loss of possible independence caused by membership. On 5 June 1975 the new Labour government of Harold Wilson therefore held Britain's first-ever referendum – a direct vote in which the entire electorate is asked to vote on a particular question. People were asked whether they wanted to remain in the EEC. With a turnout of 25,903,194 (64.5%), the electorate decided by 17,378,581 votes (67.23%) to 8,470,073 (32.77%) to remain in Europe. The debate about Britain's role in Europe was over, at least for the time being.

⭐ The count gets underway after the 1975 referendum to decide whether Britain will remain in the EEC.

> 66 *Parliament has decided to consult the electorate on the question of whether Britain should remain in the European Economic Community. Do you want Britain to remain in the EEC?* 99

Referendum question, 5 June 1975

Although the 1975 referendum supported Britain's continuing membership of the EEC, as it then was, many people did not accept the result. They remained opposed to membership and disliked the European project.

★ Margaret Thatcher addressing the College of Europe in Bruges on 20 September 1988.

POLITICAL DIVISIONS

Opposition to the EEC came from those in the Conservative Party who believed Britain's future lay with the countries of the Commonwealth (former territories of the British Empire), not Europe. They supported Britain as an independent nation and objected to the loss of power and authority to the EU headquarters in Brussels. On the opposite side of the political spectrum, left-wing members of the Labour Party objected to the fact that the EEC was pro-capitalist and prevented them from establishing a socialist economy in Britain. Only the small, centre Liberal Party was united in support of European union.

MRS THATCHER

The Conservative government led by Margaret Thatcher between 1979 and 1990 became increasingly anti-European. Mrs Thatcher supported the Single European Act of 1986, which introduced a free market in goods and services across Europe (see p.13) because she believed in free trade. However, she objected to moves to tie the different European currencies together and create a European central bank. In particular she was strongly opposed to giving more powers to Brussels. In a famous speech to the College of Europe in Bruges, Belgium, in 1988, she stated that the best way to build a European Union was through the 'willing and active co-operation between independent states,' not by creating a European superstate.

> 66 *We have not successfully rolled back the frontiers of the state in Britain, only to see them reimposed at a European level, with a European superstate exercising a new dominance from Brussels.* 99

–Margaret Thatcher, 20 September 1988

★ While the Conservative Party under Margaret Thatcher opposed much European legislation, the opposition Labour Party liked the protection it gave to EU workers.

THE OTHER SIDE

As the Conservatives became more opposed to the direction the European Union was taking, the Labour Party became more in favour. It liked the social provisions of the Union that supported workers' rights, notably the introduction of a maximum 48-hour working week. However, the Labour government led by Tony Blair that took power in 1997 kept Britain out of the euro, while supporting other aspects of EU policy.

THE EUROPEAN COMMISSION

Along with the Parliament and the Council, the European Commission was set up in the 1950s under the EU's founding treaties. The Commission manages the daily running of the EU and the spending of EU funds. It proposes new laws and makes sure everyone obeys the rules. If not, it can take rule-breakers to the EU Court of Justice. It is often called the 'guardian of the treaties'.

EU COMMISSION FACT SHEET

- It is based in the Belgian capital, Brussels
- There are 28 commissioners, one from each member state
- National governments put commissioners forward, but their selection has to be approved by the European Parliament
- Each commissioner handles a specific area of EU policy, from trade to agriculture
- He or she needs to look after the interests of the EU as a whole, not just those of his or her home country
- There is also a Commission president, chosen from the 28 commissioners by EU member states and approved by the Parliament
- The president and commissioners serve a five-year term. They are in power at the same time as members of the European Parliament
- The Commission represents the EU on the world stage
- Behind the scenes, 24,000 civil servants help the Commission carry out its work

TRIANGLE OF POWER

The European Commission, the European Parliament and the European Council together make up an 'institutional triangle' (see p.39). All of the EU member states' national governments have handed over some of their power to these institutions, and expect them to do what is best for the EU as a whole. These institutions are most powerful and successful when they all work closely together and trust one another, but this is not always easy to achieve.

★ The Austrian commissioner Johannes Hahn is responsible for negotiations with nations wanting to become EU members.

SCANDAL IN THE COMMISSION

If the European Parliament is not happy with the work of the commissioners, it can vote to sack every one of them (but not individuals). This almost happened in 1999, when several commissioners were accused of appointing close friends and of handling funds badly. All the members resigned before the issue came to a vote in Parliament, and the new commissioners promised to make big changes in the way they worked.

LAYING DOWN THE LAW

If member states have agreed that laws enacted by the EU as a whole will mean better results than national governments acting alone, the Commission will be the driving force behind putting those laws into action.

Areas where only the EU passes laws:
- Single market (the same trading rules for everyone)
- Customs (the rules at the EU's external borders)
- Monetary policy (for countries who have signed up to the euro)

Areas where both the EU and member states can pass laws:
- Agriculture and fisheries
- Regional funding
- Environment
- Consumer protection
- Employment and health and safety at work
- Transport
- Energy
- Public health and food safety

(But note that if the EU acts first on one aspect of these, then member states may not pass laws themselves.)

Areas where the EU can act, but member states keep the right to pass legislation:
- International development
- Research and space policy

Areas where member states have most of the responsibility, but the EU can help:
- Healthcare
- Industry
- Culture
- Tourism
- Education

(For example: the EU will not tell you how to run your local hospital, but it will run campaigns against smoking.)

★ Situated in Brussels, the EU's Berlaymont building has been specially constructed as a state-of-the-art headquarters for the EU.

THE EUROPEAN PARLIAMENT

The EU Parliament is a melting pot of opinions. It is the place where Europe's elected politicians battle to balance the interests of their country with the interests of Europe as a whole, and decide if proposals from the Commission should become law.

ON THE MOVE

The European Parliament works in two places. Full meetings for elected Members of the European Parliament (MEPs) are held in the French town of Strasbourg for one week every month. The rest of the time there are committees and other meetings in Brussels. This split adds to the running costs and can be unpopular. But for France, the Strasbourg Parliament is a source of national pride. There is another location involved: the people who do the Parliament's administration are based in Luxembourg.

A BABBLE OF VOICES

Making sure everyone understands what is going on in Parliament can be a complicated business. The European Parliament is the most multilingual parliament in the world. In 2016, there are 24 different European languages to deal with, with possibly more to come. That means, in theory, at least 550 different language combinations, although in practice interpretation is usually done through English, French and German. There is also the problem of translating more than 100,000 pages of EU rules and regulations, so that, for example, British farmers, French fishermen or Polish plumbers can read about issues that concern them in their own language.

★ The European Parliament in Strasbourg has enough room for its 751 MEPs, plus at least 680 visitors.

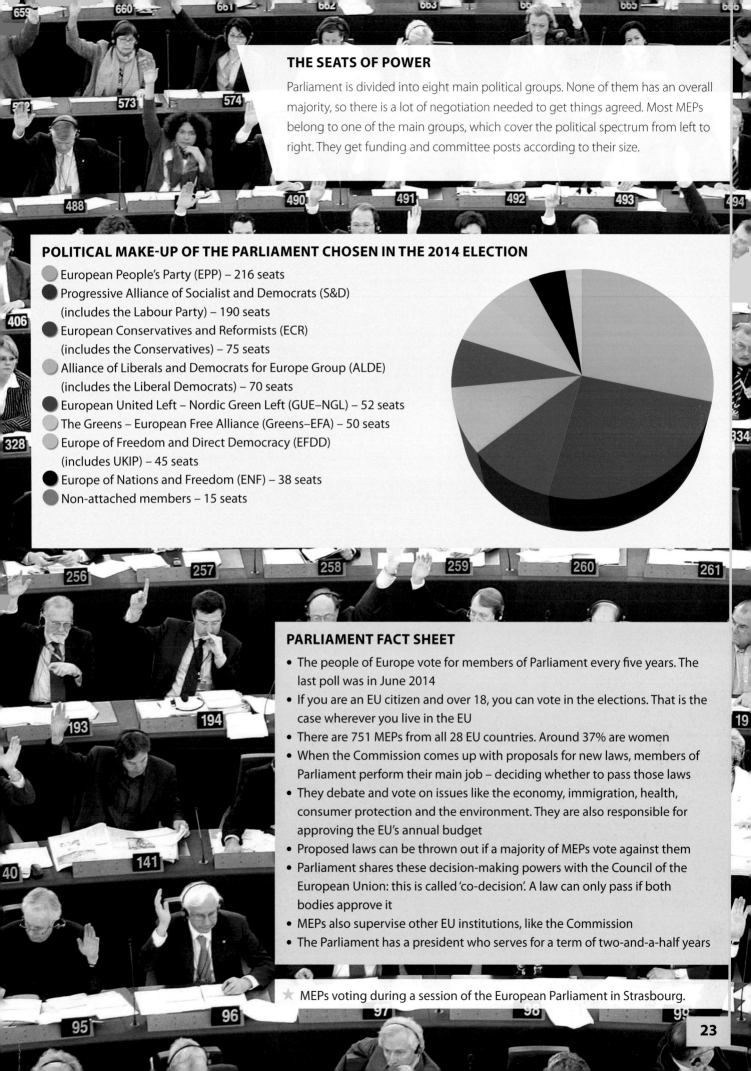

THE SEATS OF POWER

Parliament is divided into eight main political groups. None of them has an overall majority, so there is a lot of negotiation needed to get things agreed. Most MEPs belong to one of the main groups, which cover the political spectrum from left to right. They get funding and committee posts according to their size.

POLITICAL MAKE-UP OF THE PARLIAMENT CHOSEN IN THE 2014 ELECTION

- European People's Party (EPP) – 216 seats
- Progressive Alliance of Socialist and Democrats (S&D) (includes the Labour Party) – 190 seats
- European Conservatives and Reformists (ECR) (includes the Conservatives) – 75 seats
- Alliance of Liberals and Democrats for Europe Group (ALDE) (includes the Liberal Democrats) – 70 seats
- European United Left – Nordic Green Left (GUE–NGL) – 52 seats
- The Greens – European Free Alliance (Greens–EFA) – 50 seats
- Europe of Freedom and Direct Democracy (EFDD) (includes UKIP) – 45 seats
- Europe of Nations and Freedom (ENF) – 38 seats
- Non-attached members – 15 seats

PARLIAMENT FACT SHEET

- The people of Europe vote for members of Parliament every five years. The last poll was in June 2014
- If you are an EU citizen and over 18, you can vote in the elections. That is the case wherever you live in the EU
- There are 751 MEPs from all 28 EU countries. Around 37% are women
- When the Commission comes up with proposals for new laws, members of Parliament perform their main job – deciding whether to pass those laws
- They debate and vote on issues like the economy, immigration, health, consumer protection and the environment. They are also responsible for approving the EU's annual budget
- Proposed laws can be thrown out if a majority of MEPs vote against them
- Parliament shares these decision-making powers with the Council of the European Union: this is called 'co-decision'. A law can only pass if both bodies approve it
- MEPs also supervise other EU institutions, like the Commission
- The Parliament has a president who serves for a term of two-and-a-half years

⭐ MEPs voting during a session of the European Parliament in Strasbourg.

THE COUNCIL OF THE EU

The Council is where the governments of Europe are represented, and the big decisions are made. The Council shares responsibility with the EU Parliament for passing laws and approving budgets. But in an EU club that keeps getting bigger, its leaders often struggle to agree on important issues.

WHICH COUNCIL IS WHICH?

In the Council of the European Union (also known as the Council of Ministers) ministers from each EU country meet to take decisions and pass laws. Who shows up depends on what is being discussed. If it is about health, for example, the health minister attends. Most meetings are in Brussels. High-profile summit meetings attended by presidents and prime ministers are held by the European Council. The European Council meets four times a year, and may try to settle key issues that their ministers have not been able to agree on. Trying to strike deals between 28 different countries, with widely different opinions, is often tricky.

★ President of the European Council Donald Tusk and President of the European Commission Jean-Claude Juncker confer at a European Council meeting in Riga, Latvia, in May 2015.

★ Asylum seekers in a Greek camp. Asylum and immigration is one of the many issues dealt with by the Council.

TAKING A VOTE

If the Council is tackling a sensitive issue – such as taxation, asylum, immigration, foreign policy or defence – every one of the member countries must in theory agree. In fact, EU ministers and leaders rarely vote at all, as they find it is too divisive. They prefer to do things by consensus. On other topics, though, a new system of qualified majority voting introduced in 2014 is used. This means:

- 55% of the countries, which means at least 15 of the 28 members, if voting on a proposal from the European Commission or from the High Representative for Foreign Affairs, or 72%, or 20 of the countries, for other proposals, must vote in favour
- In addition, this vote must represent at least 65% of the total EU population
- To block a vote, at least four countries most vote against a proposal

This system stops the bigger EU nations ganging up together to impose their wishes.

SHARING THE POWER

Every six months, a new EU country takes a turn at holding the presidency of the EU. This means chairing meetings like the Council summits, and representing the EU on the international stage.

JUST TO CONFUSE YOU:
THE COUNCIL OF EUROPE...

… is not an EU-created institution. It was set up in 1949, before the EU was founded. There are 47 Council members and its purpose is to defend and promote human rights, the rule of law and democracy throughout Europe. In particular, it has been a watchdog on human rights in countries that broke away from the Soviet Union. Its most important ruling is the European Convention on Human Rights. If an EU citizen has run out of options on a case in their country, they can take it to the Court of Human Rights in Strasbourg.

THE RULE OF LAW

If a member state does not like a new EU law that has been passed, it cannot simply ignore it. That new law takes precedence over existing national rules, because that is what countries sign up to when they join the EU. Here are some of the bodies that try to give everyone in the EU a fair deal.

★ The European Court of Justice in Luxembourg.

THE COURT OF JUSTICE

- It makes sure that EU member states and institutions do what the law requires them to do, equally for everyone, respecting the fundamental rights of EU citizens
- It checks that national courts do not give different rulings on the same issue
- If called upon by a member state, the Court of Justice can give rulings on how to interpret EU law. For example, the French government banned imports of British beef in 1996 following of fears of BSE or 'mad cow' disease: the European Court said this broke EU rules and ordered France to follow them
- The Court of Justice is based in Luxembourg. There is one judge from each EU country, serving a term of six years

THE COURT OF AUDITORS

- The EU is funded by money from taxpayers, so the Court of Auditors tries to make sure they are getting value for money
- The Court of Auditors is based in Luxembourg, and can audit any organisation, body or company that handles EU money
- There is one member from each EU country, serving a six-year term

THE EU AND FOOTBALL: LANDMARK CASE

The Union's lawmakers have had a big influence on the world of European football. When Belgian footballer Jean-Marc Bosman won a case against his club FC Liège at the European Court of Justice in 1995, it revolutionised football across Europe. Before the Bosman ruling, clubs demanded a transfer fee when a player moved from one club to another, even if that player's contract had finished. But this was against EU employment law, because it restricted a person's freedom of movement. So now, when footballers' contracts have run out, they have the right to move to another club on a 'Bosman free transfer'.

GETTING YOUR VOICE HEARD

Along with the bigger courts, there may be another road to justice if you are an EU citizen worried about a day-to-day local issue: the Petitions Committee of the European Parliament. For example, it took up the case of a Polish baker who moved to a German town but could not set up a business there, because ancient laws allowed only a maximum of three bakers. After pressure from this EU committee, the German government changed the rules.

In 1990 Jean-Marc Bosman's footballing contract with the Belgian club RFC Liège expired. He wanted to move to the French club of Dunkerque, but Liège demanded a high transfer fee that Dunkerque would not pay. Bosman took his case to the European Court of Justice and won.

THE EUROPEAN ECONOMIC AND SOCIAL COMMITTEE

- This is known as the 'voice of civil society'. It is an advisory body with 355 members representing a wide range of interests, from employers to trade unions, from consumers to ecologists
- It must be consulted about decisions on economic and social matters

THE COMMITTEE OF THE REGIONS

- Its 350 members are often leaders of regional government, or mayors of cities
- They are consulted when EU decisions are going to have a big impact on people regionally, for example on transport or health

THE OMBUDSMAN

- The Ombudsman is an independent go-between for complaints brought by individuals against EU authorities
- Citizens of the EU can turn to the Ombudsman if they think an EU body has acted unfairly
- The Ombudsman considers issues such as discrimination, abuse of power, lack of information or refusal to give it, or unnecessary delays in resolving outstanding issues

MONEY

Money makes the EU's world go round. Striving for a strong economy is at the heart of everything the Union has achieved, and aims to achieve in the future. It wants higher standards of living for its people, because it believes that with prosperity comes peace. To do this, the EU takes from its richer members and gives to its poorer ones.

⭐ Poorer rural countries such as Romania gain more money from the EU than they put in to the central EU pot.

WHERE DOES THE MONEY COME FROM?

In 2014, the EU set a budget of around €143 billion, which is about 1% of the gross national income of the entire EU. This is roughly equal to €281 for each person in the EU.

The EU gets its money from four main sources:

- The biggest amount comes from national governments, which each contribute around 0.7% of their GNI (gross national income)
- Each country also gives around 0.3% of their VAT (value-added tax) returns
- The EU contributes its own money from customs duties on imports from outside the EU, and other sources
- The EU has other income from sources such as contributions from non-member states such as Norway for certain programmes, interest payments, fines and surpluses

In order to make the system fairer for some of the richer countries, and therefore bigger contributors, the EU gives a rebate to Britain and discounts in GNI and VAT payments to Austria, Germany, the Netherlands and Sweden.

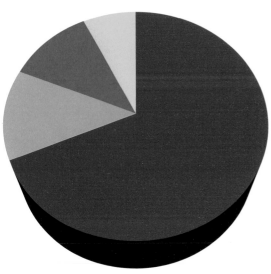

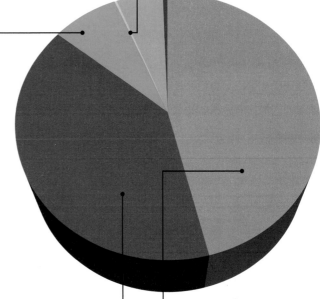

Security and citizenship includes justice, border protection, immigration and asylum, public health, consumer protection, and culture

Foreign policy includes development assistance and humanitarian aid outside the EU

SOURCES OF EU REVENUE IN 2014

● National donations	68.73%	
● VAT	12.86%	
● Own resources	11.4%	
○ Other income	6.99%	

DISHING OUT THE MONEY

The EU only spends about 6% of its budget on administration (see below). The rest goes on actual policies such as agriculture, security or culture.

EU EXPENDITURE IN 2014

Growth	49.55%
Natural resources	42.77%
Security and citizenship	8.5%
Foreign policy	0.07%
Administration	5.97%
Other	0.35%

Growth includes money for jobs, economic growth and social policies

Natural resources include the common agricultural and fisheries policies, and rural and environmental matters

MORE KEY FACTS

- The annual budget is proposed by the European Commission, discussed by the Council of the European Union and then voted on by the European Parliament
- How much you give to the EU budget depends on how big your economy is
- Germany, France, Italy and Britain contribute more than half of the EU budget
- Germany is the biggest net contributor to the budget, while Poland and Greece are the biggest beneficiaries

THE EUROPEAN INVESTMENT BANK

- It lends money at very low rates to countries in the EU and in the former Soviet Union and Mediterranean region
- Money can be used for projects like roads, bridges and water purification plants
- It is based in Luxembourg

THE EURO

In 19 member states of the EU, the currency is the same in each country. About 337 million Europeans use the same notes and coins and get more of the same money out from bank cash points whenever they cross the border from one country to another inside the EU. The euro, as this common currency is known, is one of the greatest achievements of the European Union. It is a living symbol of the European Union and all it stands for. However, the euro has not been without its problems.

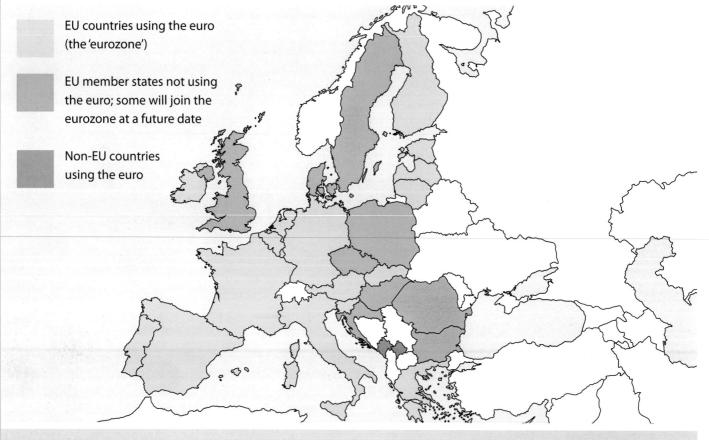

EU countries using the euro (the 'eurozone')

EU member states not using the euro; some will join the eurozone at a future date

Non-EU countries using the euro

WHO'S IN, WHO'S OUT

IN
Austria, Belgium, Cyprus, Estonia, Finland, France, Germany, Greece, Ireland, Italy, Latvia, Lithuania, Luxembourg, Malta, the Netherlands, Portugal, Slovakia, Slovenia and Spain, plus French colonies in the Caribbean, South America and Indian Ocean. In addition, the four microstates of Andorra, Monaco, San Marino and the Vatican City have agreed with the EU to use the euro. Both Kosovo and Montenegro are outside the EU, but use the euro as their currency.

OUT
Britain and Denmark have agreed a deal where they can decide to join the eurozone at a later stage. Sweden's voters rejected euro membership in a referendum in 2003.

WAITING
Bulgaria, Croatia, Czech Republic, Hungary, Poland and Romania.

One of the EU's most striking achievements is the single currency because:
- It is a world currency that makes trade easier between the nations that use it
- It allows people to travel throughout Europe without having to change money
- It is a symbol of the EU's political progress

THE EUROPEAN CENTRAL BANK – KEY FACTS

- It is based in Frankfurt, Germany
- It was set up in 1998 to introduce and manage the euro
- It decides on interest rates across the euro area (eurozone)
- It aims to keep inflation below 2%
- It is entirely independent of other EU institutions or national governments
- It is responsible for shaping and managing monetary and economic policy
- Decisions regarding it are made by the Governing Council: an Executive Board of six members, plus the governors of 19 central banks from the euro area

EURO FACTS

- The euro was first named in 1995 and was first used for accounting in 1999
- The first euro coins and banknotes came into circulation on 1 January 2002
- Today the euro is used by 337 million Europeans in 19 member states, with another 210 million people using currencies pegged or tied to the euro
- The euro is the second biggest reserve currency in the world after the US dollar
- The euro has the highest value of coins and banknotes in circulation, more than any other currency in the world
- The eurozone is the second largest economy in the world after the USA

SUCCESS OR FAILURE?

In simple terms, the euro has been a great success. It is the world's first major currency union and has survived for 14 years. Recent member countries of the EU are steadily joining it. However, the euro has faced some substantial problems. The eurozone is a currency union, not an economic union. All the countries share a common currency but their central banks are separate and their economies are different sizes and have very different needs. A single currency and exchange rate means that some eurozone countries can no longer sell their goods abroad because they are too expensive. A single interest rate does not work for both rich and poor countries, as the cost of borrowing money is often wrong for some countries. As a result, rich countries like Germany benefit from the euro, while poor countries like Greece and Portugal suffer with high unemployment. With the euro, it is definitely the case that one size does not fit all.

★ The ability to use one currency across 19 different European countries is much appreciated by their citizens.

Only about 5.4 per cent of people across the EU work in farming, and it accounts for only 2.3% of the EU's GDP. Yet spending on agriculture makes up around one-third of the EU budget and it is an issue that still causes furious rows among member states. Why?

DOES THE 'CAP' FIT?

The answer lies in the deal that was made in the EU's early days. France agreed to a free trade in industrial goods among the six founder members, but only if its farmers were given subsidies – extra money to make sure they had a good income. The agreement is known as the 'Common Agricultural Policy' (CAP). It came into play in 1962, when people still had strong memories of wartime food shortages, and wanted to avoid the same thing happening again. This is how the CAP worked: the European Community set a target price for farm goods. If the market price dropped lower, it would step in and pay the extra. But as the years went by farmers kept on producing more and more, because they knew they would get a good price for it. This led to notorious 'mountains' and 'lakes' of food and drink that no one wanted, but that member states still had to pay for in subsidies. Europe's food prices have also been some of the highest in the world.

CAP'S AIMS:

- To make farms more productive
- To ensure fair living standards for the agricultural community
- To stabilise markets
- To ensure food is available
- To provide food at reasonable prices (from the Treaty of Rome)

★ French farmers protest against changes to their EU financial support in Paris in 2009.

★ Barnacle geese are among the many endangered species protected by EU regulations.

CHANGING DIRECTION

There has been a lot of talk about reforming CAP, but change only really began in the 1990s and it is still going slowly. One of the main aims has been to give more aid to farmers for things like food safety, animal welfare and looking after the environment, rather than for how much they produce. Critics of CAP say it is much too expensive and only benefits a minority of people. Supporters argue that it helps rural communities, where more than half of EU citizens live. They say it also preserves the traditional look of the countryside.

THE ENVIRONMENT

The EU has a wide-ranging set of policies about the environment. European ministers meet regularly in the Environment Council to agree common measures and standards. Among the more successful EU policies in this area is the Water Framework Directive, which ensures good quality water in lakes, rivers and around coasts. As part of this, the EU supports the Blue Flag scheme that shows that a beach or marina is clean and the water is clean enough to swim in. The EU Birds Directive protects wild birds and their habitats, while the Habitat Directive sets up special areas of conservation for protected species. Overall, the EU has now pledged to ensure sustainable development in all its policies and in total, it has established more than five hundred policies concerned with protecting and improving the environment. It has also pledged to reduce greenhouse gas emissions by 40% by 2030 (compared to 1990 emissions) to help tackle climate change, and is aiming to increase energy efficiency by 27% by the same year.

CITIZENS OF THE EU

Most people would agree that life in Europe has become more prosperous and peaceful in the years since the EU began, although not everyone would agree that this is mainly because of the EU.

According to an official 'Eurobarometer' survey in May 2015, 41% of people in the European Union have a positive image of the EU, while 19% have a negative image. The other 38% are neutral. In addition, 40% of people trust the EU, while only 31% trust their national governments. However, only 42% of people think their voice counts in the EU, while 50% think it does not.

⭐ Hungarian migrant workers on site in the Netherlands. EU citizens have the right to move to – and work in – other countries of the Union.

GETTING CLOSER, BUT KEEPING A DISTANCE

For some people, the EU can still seem like a big, remote, confusing organisation, where governments and experts make plans that have little to do with their everyday lives.

So the challenge for the EU is to strike a balance. It needs to be an effective organisation that makes the best use of its powers, but still lets people in each member state feel unique.

SYMBOLS OF EU CITIZENSHIP

Flag: five-pointed stars in a crown. There are 12 stars, a number representing perfection and completeness.

Anthem: Beethoven's Ninth Symphony, with the words of Schiller's 'Ode to Joy'.

Day: Europe Day is on 9 May, to mark the birth date of Robert Schuman, one of the the main founders of the EU (see p.11).

ROBERT
SCHUMAN
1886 — 1963

Driving licence: you can drive anywhere in the EU if you have a licence from one of the member states.

Passport: 'European Union' is written at the top, the name of the member state follows. It is burgundy red and the same size for everyone.

KNOWING YOUR RIGHTS

If you live in an EU country, you are a citizen of the European Union, and these are some of your basic rights: you can move freely between EU countries, and live in any EU nation you choose; from the age of 18, you can vote and stand in local government and European Parliament elections in the country where you live; you can receive health care, social security and social assistance throughout the EU; if you believe the EU has not been fair to you, you can take your case to the European Ombudsman.

FROM 'GOODBYE BENDY BANANAS' TO 'TOYS FOR PIGS'

The media in Eurosceptic – that is wary of or against the EU – nations like Britain are fond of finding headlines that suggest the bureaucrats of Brussels are ruling people's lives with crazy new laws. According to reports in British newspapers, for instance, the EU was going to ban bananas or cucumbers that were too bendy, and make farmers give toys to their pigs to keep them happy. The EU says the media often get the facts wrong, and devotes a whole corner of its official website to correcting mistakes. Bendy bananas and strict pig farmers, it says, are not in their sights.

★ Demonstrators take to the streets of Berlin, Germany in 2015 to protest against a potential EU trade deal with the USA.

THE EU AND THE WORLD

The European Union wants to play a leading role on the world stage, and wherever it can it tries to speak with one voice. But while the EU is a force to be reckoned with in the global economy, it has much less impact on world politics. So some critics call it 'an economic giant but a political dwarf'. It also lacks a figurehead in the form of a leader who can tell the world what the EU thinks. As US diplomat Henry Kissinger famously asked in the 1970s: 'If I want to talk to Europe, who do I phone?'

TRADING UP

- The EU is the world's largest free-trade area, and accounts for about one-quarter of global imports and exports
- The EU and its member states together give 41 per cent of the world's development aid
- Together the United States and the EU represent 60 per cent of the world's GDP, 33 per cent of its trade in goods, and 42 per cent of its trade in services. The two are discussing setting up the Transatlantic Trade and Investment Partnership to create the world's largest free trade area
- The EU is one of China's top trading partners, and business is growing
- The EU keeps close links with its former colonies: countries in Africa, the Caribbean and the Pacific (known as the ACP). Seventy-nine countries are now in the ACP, and and can sell their goods to the EU without paying any duties

TALKING POLITICS

For the EU, it can be difficult to speak with one voice on issues such as defence and foreign policy. That is because member states have kept the right to decide these issues for themselves, and often disagree on what to do. There were big disputes, for example, over the invasion of Iraq in 2003. In 1999, the EU appointed Javier Solana, a former secretary general of NATO, as its first foreign policy chief. His current successor is Federica Mogherini, former foreign minister of Italy. She is the person meant to speak for Europe on international affairs, but she can only speak when all the 28 EU government agree, which is not always the case. The backbone of the EU's approach to world affairs is the Common Foreign and Security Policy (CFSP). It deals with issues like peace, security, international co-operation, democracy, human rights and rule of law. EU leaders do find common cause wherever they can. The EU holds regular summit meetings with other big countries or world organisations like the United Nations. It tries to strike deals on key world issues, from poverty to terrorism. The EU is also one of the 'Quartet', along with the United States, Russia and the United Nations, trying to bring peace to the Middle East.

★ EU foreign policy chief Federica Mogherini has been involved in trying to end the war in Ukraine and reaching agreement with Iran over its nuclear arms policies.

KEEPING THE PEACE

- EU countries decide for themselves how to organise their armed forces and whether to keep nuclear weapons as a deterrent
- Most EU countries (22 out of 28) belong to NATO, the North Atlantic Treaty Organisation. It was formed in 1949 by countries in Europe and North America, to protect against a possible attack by the Soviet Union. Today its aims are to defend democracy and freedom, and to push for peace and stability
- Neither the EU or NATO have their own armies, but member states can send troops under the banner of either. The two organisations work closely together in crisis situations, and the EU can send peacekeepers if NATO does not want to, as happened in the Democratic Republic of Congo in 2003
- EU troops and police, collectively known as EUFOR, have also been sent on peacekeeping missions to Bosnia–Herzegovina, Macedonia, Afghanistan, Chad and the Central African Republic. The aim is to keep a lid on further outbreaks of trouble, and to help rebuild lives and communities

An Irish Army soldier on duty in Chad, Africa in 2008 as part of the EUFOR mission.

TALKING BUSINESS

Unity is easier in matters of trade, because member states have handed over all their negotiating powers to the EU Commission. They believe they will get the best deal if they stick together.

At meetings of the World Trade Organization, for example, the EU says its aim is to push for fair and equal access to markets around the world, and to persuade others to stick to the rules. However, critics say that the EU's own rules on protecting its farmers get in the way of free trade.

SUPPLYING AID

The EU is also a major provider of overseas aid. In 2013 it gave €1.35 billion in aid, helping 124 million people in 90 non-EU countries. About 40% went to Africa, 18% to Asia, Latin America, the Caribbean and Pacific, and 32% to the Middle East and the Mediterranean. The aid is used for food, shelter, health, water supplies and preparation for possible disasters.

TAKING STOCK

The world has never seen a political project as grand and bold as the European Union. It is unique for so many nation-states to hand over so much of their sovereignty. The EU itself has many of the symbols of a nation: it has a flag, an anthem, a currency and a single market. It keeps expanding both its size and its ambitions. As it tries to come up with more common policy on foreign and security affairs, it may look even more like a single nation.

KNOWING WHO YOU ARE

Each country still keeps much of what makes it unique. The French have not become less French because they are in the EU, and neither have the British become less British. A lot is still decided by how the big countries in Western Europe – Britain, France and Germany – get along. But countries in Eastern Europe, like Poland, are playing a more and more important role.

★ Balloons are released at the Brandenburg Gate in Berlin, Germany to mark the expansion of the EU on 1 May 2004.

THE EU'S INSTITUTIONS IN ACTION

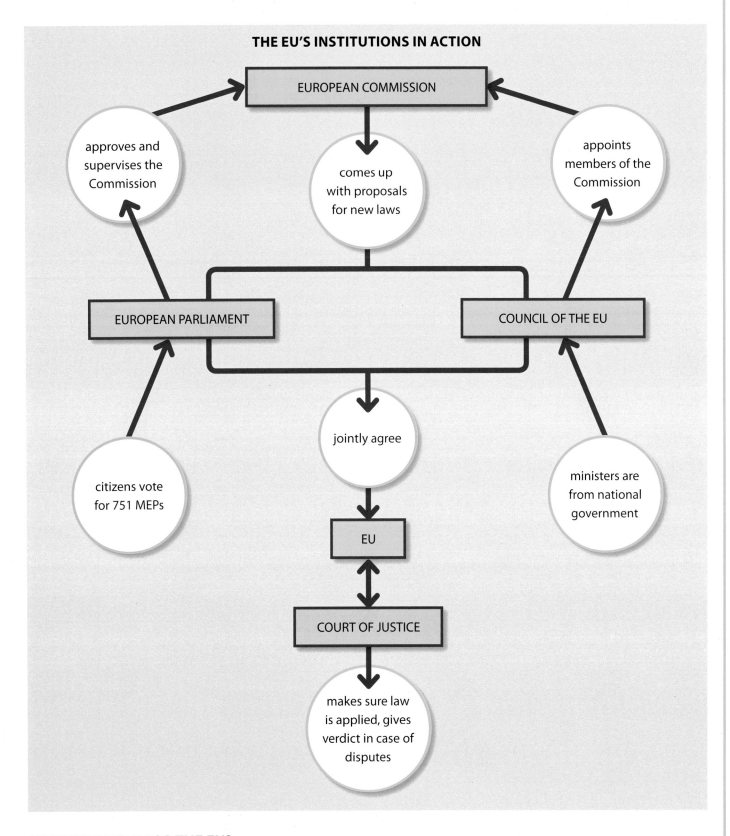

SO WHERE NOW FOR THE EU?

The questions that will continue to challenge the European Union of the future are the same ones that have puzzled it in the past. How much power do member states want to hand over to the EU, and how can they reach agreement when there are so many different points of view? Such questions are at the heart of every dispute, on everything from a 'yes-or-no' vote on the EU constitution, to a battle over whether a Polish plumbing business is allowed to offer the same services in Paris as it does in Warsaw. Even when there is a verdict on an issue, it is rarely a simple one, and different people read it in different ways, depending on where their interest lies.

FACING THE FUTURE

The European Union is now in its seventh decade. This makes it the most successful political union and the longest lasting free trade area in the world. It currently has 28 members, but if all its potential new members join, that number will rise to 35. Virtually the entire European continent west of Russia will be a member. But the very size of the EU brings with it some very profound questions about the Union itself.

WIDE OR DEEP?

When the EU began in the 1950s, it only had six members. They were linked geographically by the River Rhine and to the south by the Mediterranean. All had emerged deeply scarred by the Second World War. They sought to work closely together to overcome their problems. They believed in a political union of European countries in which national sovereignty would be shared. As the Union has grown, that vision has changed. Britain joined to become part of a larger trading area and to support the creation of a single market in goods and services throughout Europe. It has never supported a political union of Europe. The new members from Central Europe and the

Balkans wanted to join to make their countries richer and to act as a bulwark against Russia, which had previously dominated them through their communist governments. Different countries want different things from the Union. The question now facing the EU is how it will cope with such large numbers of member countries wanting different outcomes from their membership. Will it become a wide union of free trade and a single market supported by free and independent states, or a deep political union in which each country gives up much of its independence and power to Brussels?

★ One potential new member of the EU is Turkey, but is the Union ready to accept the world's seventh most populous Muslim nation as a member?

⭐ Violent protests erupted in Greece in 2012 against the Greek government's proposed austerity measures (see below).

HOW BIG?

If the European Union expands to take in all its eight new potential members:
- It will stretch from the Arctic Circle to the Mediterranean and from the Atlantic to the Caucasus Mountains in central Asia
- Its total population will rise from 508 million to 605 million people on present-day figures
- Only seven European countries will remain outside it (including Britain).

THE EURO

In straightforward terms, the euro has been a success. People in 19 countries now use the same notes and coins. They don't need to exchange their money for a new currency when they cross most European national borders. This also makes economic sense for businesses, as exporters and importers of goods don't have to pay the cost of changing currencies and can price their goods using the same currency across Europe.

However, the euro has in some ways created economic turmoil. Because the national economies are so different,

some richer states, such as Germany, have prospered while poorer nations, such as Greece, have suffered. Poorer countries can no longer sell their goods cheaply because they no longer control their exchange rates. In addition, a worldwide financial crisis that began in the United States in 2008 soon spread to Europe. Banks in Portugal, Spain, Ireland and elsewhere had lent too much money and had to be bailed out by their governments. This meant that governments ran up huge debts and found it difficult to borrow more money to run their economies. As a result, they had to raise taxes and cut services, hurting working people. This crisis has harmed the stability of the euro.

MIGRATION

The European Union has always been a magnet for migrants seeking work and a better life. For years, immigrants from Africa have tried to enter the Union in boats across the Mediterranean Sea, but their numbers were comparatively small. In 2015 however, a new wave of immigrants from Syria threatened to overwhelm the EU.

⭐ Many of the refugees are single children who have lost their families because of war.

THE SYRIAN WAR

In 2011 protests broke out in Syria against the government of President Bashar al–Assad. The government responded with force, leading to violent civil war. Civilians were bombed and gassed in their homes, with thousands killed and many more injured. The fighting intensified when the Islamic State of Iraq and the Levant or ISIS, a militant Islamic group, seized large parts of the country. About 6.5 million Syrians fled their homes. Some moved to safer parts of their country while 4 million fled into neighbouring Lebanon, Jordan or Turkey. From there they began to find their way into the EU. These refugees were often joined by people fleeing war in Iraq and Afghanistan or repression in Eritrea.

The main entry points into the EU were by boat from Turkey to the Greek islands or from Egypt or Libya across the Mediterranean into Italy. In 2015 the trickle of refugees turned into a flood. More than 100,000 people crossed into the EU in July 2015 alone, with 8,000 arriving each day. By the end of the year, more than one million refugees had arrived.

⭐ During the summer of 2015, more than 8,000 refugees were arriving in the EU each day.

THE EU REACTS

The EU's response to this crisis was muddled. The existing Dublin Regulation says that refugees must claim asylum at their point of arrival in the Union. If they try to move to another country illegally, they are then returned to their point of entry. Many refugees however took advantage of the Schengen Agreement (see box) and started to move across the open borders towards Germany. In response, Hungary and other countries closed their borders, while Germany abandoned the Dublin Regulation and stated it would register refugees when they crossed the German border.

With the Dublin Regulation and the Schengen Agreement both in tatters, the EU tried to get more countries to accept refugees. Many, however, refused. A proposal to set up an EU border force to police the EU's frontiers was opposed by those states that did not want to lose their national right to control their boundaries. Germany, Austria and Sweden, which had accepted more than 90 % of the refugees, accused Greece of not policing its own borders properly.

This crisis will continue as long as the Syrian war continues. The EU has proved itself unable to cope, with member states openly arguing with each other. It is one of the biggest crises the EU has ever faced.

THE SCHENGEN AGREEMENT

The Schengen Agreement is a treaty which allows people to travel freely across the Schengen Area, without any border controls. Currently 26 countries participate in the Schengen Area, with a total population of over 400 million and an area of 4.3 million sq km.

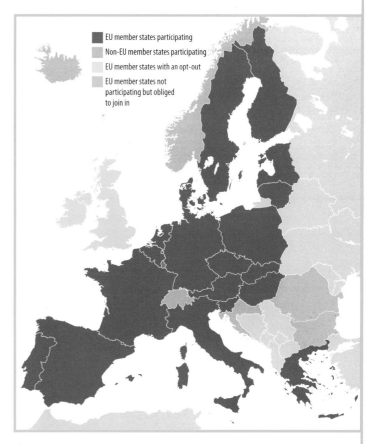

⭐ The Schengen Agreement on open borders operates throughout most of the EU.

BRITAIN'S REFERENDUM

In Britain, divisions over its membership of the European Union came to a head on 23 June 2016, when a referendum was held to decide whether Britain should remain in or leave the EU. The result, when it was announced in the early hours of Friday 24 June, came as a huge shock.

★ In early 2016, David Cameron successfully renegotiated some of Britain's terms of membership with the EU before announcing the date of the referendum and starting the campaign to remain in the EU.

THE REFERENDUM

During the referendum campaign, the prime minister David Cameron, and most of his Conservative government supported Britain's continuing membership of the EU. They were joined by: Labour, the Liberal Democrats, the Welsh and Scottish nationalist parties, and all the Northern Irish parties except the Democratic Unionists. The 'Brexit' or Leave side was headed by: Boris Johnson, the former mayor of London; Michael Gove, the Justice Secretary; other leading Conservatives, a few Labour MPs, and the United Kingdom Independence Party (UKIP), led by Nigel Farage. Cabinet members opposed to membership were allowed to speak out even if that meant arguing against their own government.

> **66** *Should Britain remain a member of the European Union or leave the European Union?* **99**

Referendum question put to the British electorate, 23 June 2016

IN?
- The EU brings peace and prosperity to Europe
- The EU Single Market makes it easier and cheaper for UK companies to sell their products in Europe, creating jobs
- The Single Market makes travel cheaper across the EU; for example, roaming charges for mobile phone calls will be abolished across the EU in 2017
- The EU buys 44% of everything we sell abroad
- British taxpayers only contribute about 1p in every £ towards the cost of the EU
- EU membership allows UK police forces to use intelligence from other EU nations
- Britain will not have to use the euro, has opted out of any commitment to further political unification in Europe, and will keep control of its borders

OUT?
- Britain would become an independent nation again
- Britain would regain its sovereignty from Brussels
- Britain would not have to obey foreign, European laws
- Britain would regain full control over its borders
- Britain could negotiate free-trade deals with countries around the world
- Britain would not have to pay the EU any more money

★ The campaign bus for the Leave side, which advertised a promise to spend the money currently spent on the EU on the NHS instead. Both sides clashed over a range of issues, but immigration was one of the biggest.

THE RESULT

Few people predicted the outcome of the referendum, which was in doubt until the very end. The actual result was clear, but showed wide regional variations.

	LEAVE	REMAIN
UNITED KINGDOM	17,410,742 **(51.9%)**	16,141,241 **(48.1%)**
	26,033 people spoiled their ballot papers	
ENGLAND	15,188,406 **(53.4%)**	13,266,996 **(46.6%)**
LONDON	1,513,23 **(40.1%)**	2,263,519 **(59.9%)**
WALES	854,572 **(52.5%)**	772,347 **(47.5%)**
SCOTLAND	1,018,322 **(38%)**	1,661,191 **(62%)**
NORTHERN IRELAND	349,442 **(44.2%)**	440,707 **(55.8%)**
TURNOUT	33,578,016 people **(72.2%)** voted out of a total electorate of 46,501,241	

Britain therefore divided into two, with Wales and most of England voting to leave, and London, Scotland and Northern Ireland voting to remain. The vote also divided the generations, with an estimated 75% of 18–24-year-olds and 56% of 25–49-year-olds voting to remain, while 56% of 50–64-year olds and 61% of those over 65 voted to leave.

THE OUTCOME

David Cameron resigned as prime minister as soon as the result was announced. His successor, Theresa May, became Britain's new leader in July 2016. The pound fell in value and the new political uncertainty caused concerns about jobs and the British economy.

In order to leave the European Union, a member government has to invoke Article 50 of the 2007 Lisbon Treaty. This gives the leaving member two years to negotiate the new terms of its relationship with the EU before its membership ends. This time period can be extended if every EU member country agrees. Among the many items to be discussed are trade, the single market and the free movement of people. These negotiations are likely to be difficult for Britain, as the Leave campaign had not stated its terms on which Britain would leave the EU, and few in government expected the Leave campaign to win.

Britain is still part of Europe and although it is expected that Britain will cease to be a member of the European Union after 2018, its relationship with the EU will still be important and decisions and policies made by the EU will continue to affect Britain.

EU MEMBER STATES: FACTFILES

FRANCE

Capital: Paris
Population: 66,627,602
Population growth rate: 0.45%
Median age: 40.9 years
Life expectancy at birth: 79.3 years for men, 85.5 years for women
Total land area: 543, 965 sq km (the largest in Western Europe)
Border countries: Andorra, Belgium, Germany, Italy, Luxembourg, Monaco, Spain, Switzerland
Coastline: 3,427 km
Ethnic groups: French and other European 85%, North African 10%, Black 3.3%, Asian 1.7%
Religions: Roman Catholic 50%, Protestant 8%, other Christian 2%, Jewish 1%, Muslim 8%, others 21%
Government type: Republic: presidential democracy. President elected by popular vote every five years. A bicameral (two-chamber) parliament is made up of the Senate and National Assembly. The president names the prime minister
Administration: France has 13 metropolitan regions (including Corsica) and five overseas regions: French Guiana, Guadeloupe, Martinique, Mayotte and Réunion are part of the French Republic and part of the EU
Economy: France is the sixth-largest economy in the world and the third in Europe after Germany and Britain
GDP: $2.83 trillion, made up of agriculture 1.9%, industry 18.3%, services 79.8%
Industries: Machinery, chemicals, automobiles, metallurgy, aircraft, electronics, textiles, food processing, tourism
Labour force: 30 million
Unemployment: 10%
Currency: Euro
Calling code: +33
Language: French. There are also several regional languages
France in the EU: A founder member with 74 MEPs; France voted 'no' in a referendum on the EU constitution in 2005
France in the world: Founding member of the UN; one of the five permanent members of the UN Security Council; one of only nine nuclear powers; NATO member; world's number one tourist destination

GERMANY

Capital: Berlin
Population: 81,459,000
Population growth rate: −0.18%
Median age: 46.1 years
Life expectancy at birth: 77.9 years for men, 82.6 years for women
Total land area: 357,027 sq km
Border countries: Denmark, Poland, Czech Republic, Austria, Switzerland, France, Luxembourg, Belgium, the Netherlands (more than any other European country)
Coastline: 2,389 km
Ethnic groups: German 80%, other European 11.6%, Turk 3.7%, Asian 1.7%, other 2.8%
Religions: Roman Catholic 30.8%, Protestant 30.3%, Orthodox 1.3%, Jewish 0.1%, Muslim 2.7%, other 34.8%
Government type: Federal republic, parliamentary democracy. The power is divided between the federation and the 16 individual states. A bicameral parliament is made up of the Federal Assembly (Bundestag) and the Federal Council (Bundesrat)
Administration: 16 states, divided into 402 districts
Economy: Europe's largest, but has grown slowly in recent years. Germany's population is ageing and integration with the former East Germany has been a challenge
GDP: $3.84 trillion, made up of agriculture 1%, industry 28%, services 71%
Industries: Iron and steel, cement, coal, chemicals, plastics, machinery, vehicles, ships, aircraft, machine tools, electronics, information technology, medical supplies, pharmaceuticals, food and drink, textiles
Labour force: 52.9 million
Unemployment: 4.7%
Currency: Euro
Calling code: +49
Language: German. There are also minor regional languages and the immigrant languages of Turkish, Kurdish, Polish, Arabic and Russian
Germany in the EU: A founder member with 96 MEPs; Europe's most populous nation and most powerful economy; East and West Germany reunified in 1990
Germany in the world: One of the world's leading industrialised nations; member state of the UN, NATO; pushing for permanent membership of UN Security Council

ITALY

Capital: Rome
Population: 60,795,612
Population growth rate: 0.34%
Median age: 44.2 years
Life expectancy at birth: 79.3 years for men, 84.7 years for women
Land area: 301,338 sq km
Border countries: Austria, France, Holy See (Vatican City), San Marino, Slovenia, Switzerland
Coastline: 7,600 km
Ethnic groups: Italian 91%, other Europeans 5%, North African 1.5%, others 2.5%
Religions: Roman Catholic 87%, other Christian 2%, Muslim 1.8%, other 9%
Government type: Democratic republic. Bicameral parliament consisting of Chamber of Deputies and Senate. There is a separate judiciary and an executive branch with a Council of Ministers (cabinet) headed by the prime minister. The president of the republic is elected for seven years, and nominates the prime minister. Several dozen governments since the Second World War
Administration: 20 regions; five have special autonomous status
Economy: Industrial north with many private companies. South is more dependent on welfare and agriculture
GDP: $2.17 trillion, made up of agriculture 2%, industry 24%, services 74%
Industries: Tourism, machinery, chemicals, iron and steel, food processing, textiles, motor vehicles, clothing, footwear, ceramics
Labour force: 25.7 million
Unemployment: 11.3%
Currency: Euro
Calling code: +39
Languages: Italian, French, German and Slovene spoken in some areas, and many dialects
Italy in the EU: A founder member; 73 MEPs
Italy in the world: Rich cultural history and home to largest number of UNESCO World Heritage sites (51); NATO member; long coastline is magnet for illegal immigrants from North Africa and southeast Europe

THE NETHERLANDS

Capital: Amsterdam
Population: 16,971,452
Population growth rate: 0.44%
Median age: 42.1 years
Life expectancy at birth: 78.9 years for men, 83.2 for women
Total land area: 41,526 sq km (of which almost 20% is water)
Border countries: Belgium and Germany
Coastline: 451 km
Ethnic groups: Dutch 78.6%, other European 5.9%, Turk 2.4%, Indonesian 2.2%, Moroccan 2.2%, Surinamese 2.1%, other 6.6%
Religions: Roman Catholic 23.7%, Protestant 10.2%, Muslim 5%, other 6%, no religion 55.1%
Government type: Constitutional monarchy, government based in the Hague. The monarch is the head of state and formally appoints the government, which is historically always a coalition because no single party has enough support to take charge. The prime minister heads the government. Parliament consists of two houses: the First and Second Chamber
Administration: 12 provinces
Economy: A modern industrialised nation; exports a large number of agricultural products; a European transport hub
GDP: $881 billion, made up of agriculture 2.8%, industry 24.1%, services 73.2%
Industries: Mostly food processing, chemicals, petroleum refining, electrical machinery; has one of the world's largest natural gas fields; modern farming system
Labour force: 7.75 million
Unemployment: 8.2%
Currency: Euro
Calling code: +31
Languages: Dutch, Frisian
The Netherlands in the EU: Founder member; 26 MEPs; Dutch voted 'no' in a referendum on the EU Constitution in 2005
The Netherlands in the world: Often known as Holland, although this is the name of a region in the west of the country; one of the world's most densely populated, flattest and low lying nations (the name means 'low country'); NATO member; famous for windmills, dykes, tulips, clogs and liberal views on drugs and prostitution; hosts the International Court of Justice

BELGIUM

Capital: Brussels
Population: 11,190,845
Population growth rate: 0.82%
Median age: 43.1 years
Life expectancy at birth: 76.8 years for men, 83.2 years for women
Total land area: 30,528 sq km
Border countries: France, Germany, Luxembourg, the Netherlands
Coastline: 66.5 km
Ethnic groups: Fleming 57%, Walloon 37%, other 6%
Religions: Roman Catholic 58%, other Christian 7%, Muslim 5%, other 2%, no religion 28%
Government type: Federal parliamentary democracy under a constitutional monarch. The king is head of state and formally appoints the prime minister and the cabinet. A bicameral parliament consists of a Senate and a Chamber of Deputies. There are now three levels of government (federal, regional and linguistic community) with a complex share of power. Belgium is one of the few countries where, by law, people must vote, so turnout in elections is high
Administration: 10 provinces and 3 regions (Flanders, Wallonia and Brussels)
Economy: One of the most highly industrialised places in the world; few natural resources; Belgium has a modern transport network; about 75% of its trade is with other EU countries
GDP: $527.8 billion, made up of agriculture 1.3%, industry 16.6%, services 80.1%
Industries: Engineering and metal products, motor vehicle assembly, transport equipment, scientific instruments, processed food and drink, chemicals, basic metals, textiles, glass, petroleum
Labour force: 5.25 million
Unemployment: 8.5%
Currency: Euro
Calling code: +32
Languages: Bilingual: Dutch 60%, French 40%, German (official) less than 1%
Belgium in the EU: Founder member; 21 MEPs; at the crossroads of Western Europe; most western European countries are within 1,000 km of Brussels
Belgium in the world: Famous for being the home of both the European Union and NATO, for its huge numbers of international diplomats and bureaucrats, and for its chocolate and beer

LUXEMBOURG

Capital: Luxembourg
Population: 562,958
Population growth rate: 1.12%
Median age: 39.6 years
Life expectancy at birth: 75.8 years for men, 82.5 years for women
Total land area: 2,586 sq km
Border countries: Belgium, France, Germany
Coastline: 0 km (landlocked)
Ethnic groups: Luxembourger 55.5%, other 44.5%
Religions: Roman Catholic 68.7%, Protestant 3.7%, other 2.6%, no religion 25%
Government type: Parliamentary, with a constitutional monarchy. A cabinet of ministers is recommended by the prime minister and appointed by the monarch, the Grand Duke. Parliament consists of the Chamber of Deputies Administration: the Grand Duchy of Luxembourg is made up of three districts
Economy: People in Luxembourg have the second highest standard of living in the world (per capita income is $90,400). The economy was once dominated by steel manufacturing but today Luxembourg is best known as a tax haven and a centre for banking
GDP: $50 billion, made up of agriculture 2.2%, industry 17.2%, services 80.6%
Industries: Banking, iron and steel, food processing, chemicals, metal products, engineering, tyres, glass, aluminium, information technology, tourism
Labour force: 368,400, of whom 154,900 are foreign workers crossing the border from France, Germany and Belgium to work each day
Unemployment: 6%
Currency: Euro
Calling code: +352
Languages: Luxembourgish (national language). German and French (administrative languages)
Luxembourg in the EU: One of the smallest countries in Europe; a founder member of the EU, and entered into the 'Benelux Customs Union' with Belgium and the Netherlands in 1948; 6 MEPs
Luxembourg in the world: Founder member of NATO, famous for its financial and political stability

DENMARK

Capital: Copenhagen
Population: 5,699,220
Population growth rate: 0.28%
Median age: 40.5 years
Life expectancy at birth: 76 years for men, 80.8 years for women
Total land area: 43,094 sq km
Border countries: Germany
Coastline: 7,314 km
Ethnic groups: Danish 88%, other 12%
Religions: Protestant 80%, Muslim 3%, other and non-believers 17%
Government type: the Kingdom of Denmark is a constitutional monarchy, with a parliament called the People's Assembly. The monarch is the chief of state, and formally appoints the prime minister, who appoints a cabinet
Administration: Five administrative regions divided into 98 municipalities. The Faroe Islands and Greenland are part of the kingdom of Denmark, but are self-governing overseas administrative divisions
Economy: Very modern. Agriculture is high-tech, and the country is able to export more food and energy than it imports. Good welfare system
GDP: $330.8 billion, made up of agriculture 4.5%, industry 19.1%, services 76.4%
Industries: Iron, steel, chemicals, textiles and clothing, food processing, machinery, transport equipment, electronics, construction, furniture, shipbuilding and refurbishment, windmills
Labour force: 2.92 million
Unemployment: 3.9%
Currency: Danish krone
Calling code: +45
Language: Danish; others: Faroese, Greenlandic (an Inuit dialect), German (small minority),and English is main second language
Denmark in the EU: Joined in 1973; 13 MEPs; Denmark chose not to sign up to some parts of the Maastricht Treaty; in September 2000, Danish people voted against making the euro the national currency
Denmark in the world: Modern prosperous country; founder member of NATO; when a Danish newspaper published a cartoon depicting the Prophet Muhammad, it sparked worldwide protests by Muslims in 2006

IRELAND

Capital: Dublin
Population: 4,581,269
Population growth rate: 1.77%
Median age: 35.7 years
Life expectancy at birth: 78 years for men, 82.6 years for women
Total land area: 70,182 sq km
Border countries: UK
Coastline: 1,448 km
Ethnic groups: Irish 84.5%, other white 9.1%, Asian 1.5%, Black 1.4%, other 23.5%
Religions: Roman Catholic 84.16%, Protestant 3.5%, Islam 1.07%, other 3.64%, no religion 7.63%
Government type: Parliamentary democracy; bicameral parliament consists of the Senate and the House of Representatives; chief of state is the president
Administration: 26 counties
Economy: Ireland has changed from a country that relied mainly on farming, to become a modern, high-tech 'Celtic Tiger', with impressive economic growth in recent years
GDP: $250.81 billion, made up of agriculture 1.6%, industry 28%, services 70.4%
Industries: Metal processing; food products, brewing, textiles, clothing; chemicals, pharmaceuticals; machinery, transport equipment, shipping, glass and crystal, software, tourism, information technology
Labour force: 2.15 million
Unemployment: 8.9%
Currency: Euro
Calling code: +353
Languages: English; Irish Gaelic spoken mainly in western areas
Ireland in the EU: Joined in 1973; 11 MEPs; covers five-sixths of the island of Ireland: the rest is known as Northern Ireland and is part of the United Kingdom
Ireland in the world: Modern, prosperous, famous for literature and music; often referred to as the 'Republic of Ireland' to distinguish it from the island of Ireland as a whole; Irish and UK governments worked closely together to reach a peace settlement for Northern Ireland in 1998, after decades of conflict between those who wanted a united Ireland, and those who wanted to stay in the United Kingdom

BRITAIN

Capital: London
Population: 64,716,000
Population growth rate: 0.6%
Median age: 40.4 years
Life expectancy at birth: 79.5 years for men, 83.2 years for women
Total land area: 244,820 sq km
Border countries: Ireland
Coastline: 12,429 km
Ethnic groups: White British or other 87.1%, Asian 6.9%, Black 3%, other 3%
Religions: Christian 59.5%, Muslim 4.4%, Hindu 1.3%, Sikh 0.7%, Jewish 0.4%, Buddhist 0.4%, other and no religion 33.3%
Government type: Constitutional monarchy. Parliament consists of the House of Commons and upper House of Lords. There has been a major move to devolve powers to Wales, Scotland and Northern Ireland
Administration: Britain is made up of England, Wales and Scotland on the island of Great Britain, and the province of Northern Ireland on the island of Ireland. It also has several overseas territories
Economy: Fifth largest economy in the world with the world's second largest inward foreign investment, Britain is noted for its financial services industries
GDP: $2.945 trillion, made up of agriculture 0.6%, industry 21%, services 78.4%
Industries: Financial services, transport, power, electronics and communications equipment, vehicles, metals and chemicals, petroleum, paper products, food processing, textiles, clothing, consumer goods
Labour force: 31.39 million
Unemployment: 5.1%
Currency: Pound sterling
Calling code: +44
Languages: English, Welsh (spoken by about 26% of the population of Wales), Scottish Gaelic, Irish, Scots, Cornish
Britain in the EU: An EU member since 1973, Britain has often had an uneasy relationship with the rest of the EU. In a referendum held in 2016 the British electorate voted to leave the EU; 73 MEPs
Britain in the world: A founder member of NATO in 1949, Britain has a permanent seat on the UN Security Council and is de facto leader of the Commonwealth

GREECE

Capital: Athens
Population: 10,955,000
Population growth rate: −0.1%
Median age: 43.5 years
Life expectancy at birth: 77.1 years for men, 82.4 years for women
Total land area: 131,940 sq km
Border countries: Albania, Bulgaria, Turkey, Macedonia
Coastline: 13,676 km
Ethnic groups: Greek 85.3%, Albanian 4%, Macedonian 1.4%, Roma 0.9%, Turk 0.8%, other 7.6%
Religions: Orthodox 97.9%, other Christian 1.6%, Muslim 0.4%, Jewish 0.1%
Government type: Parliamentary republic; unicameral parliament; chief of state is the president
Administration: 13 regions subdivided into 325 municipalities
Economy: In 2010 high levels of national debt meant that the Greek government could no longer borrow money to pay for its services; the government was forced to ask for support from the IMF, the European Central Bank and the European Commission. This led to a severe recession and high levels of unemployment and poverty
GDP: $237.97 billion, made up of agriculture 3.5%, industry 15.9%, services 80.6%
Industries: Shipping, tourism, food processing, textiles, chemicals, mining
Labour force: 4.81 million
Unemployment: 24.5%
Currency: Euro
Calling code: +30
Language: Greek
Greece in the EU: Joined in 1981; receives a big slice of EU's aid budget; 21 MEPs
Greece in the world: Many people call it the cradle of civilisation, the birthplace of democracy. Has a rich historical and cultural heritage: Greece's literature, philosophy, art and politics are famous throughout the world. Long history of disputes with neighbour Turkey over territory in the Aegean and the divided island of Cyprus. NATO member. Greece hosted the Olympic Games in 2004

SPAIN

Capital: Madrid
Population: 46,439,864
Population growth rate: –0.5%
Median age: 41.6 years
Life expectancy at birth: 78.8 years for men, 85.2 years for women
Total land area: 505,988 sq km
Border countries: Andorra, France, Gibraltar, Portugal, Morocco
Coastline: 4,964 km
Ethnic groups: Spanish 86%, other 14%
Religions: Roman Catholic 76.7%, other 3.3%, no religion 20%
Government type: Parliamentary monarchy; the monarch is the chief of state; the bicameral National Assembly consists of the Senate and the Congress of Deputies
Administration: 17 communities made up of 50 provinces; 2 autonomous cities
Economy: Modern industrial economy with thriving tourism sector, although the country suffers from high unemployment and high levels of public debt
GDP: $1.69 trillion, made up of agriculture 2.5%, industry 23.5%, services 74%
Industries: Textiles, clothing, footwear, food and drink, metal and chemicals, shipbuilding, cars, tourism, pharmaceuticals, medical equipment
Labour force: 22.93 million
Unemployment: 20.9%
Currency: Euro
Calling code: +34
Languages: Castilian Spanish 74%, Catalan 17%, Galician 7%, Basque 2%. Castilian is official nationwide; the other languages are official regionally
Spain in the EU: Joined in 1986; 54 MEPs; voters approved the proposed EU Constitution in a referendum in 2004
Spain in the world: At the crossroads of the Atlantic and the Mediterranean, Europe and Africa. During the 16th century, Spain was a powerful empire 'on which the Sun did not set': it spread from South and Central America to East Asia. Spanish Civil War (1936–1939) was followed by international isolation under the dictator General Franco. King Carlos led Spain back to democracy after Franco's death in 1975. NATO member

PORTUGAL

Capital: Lisbon
Population: 10,427,301
Population growth rate: –0.5%
Median age: 41.1 years
Life expectancy at birth: 78.7 years for men, 75.45 years for women
Total land area: 92,391 sq km
Border countries: Spain
Coastline: 1,793 km
Ethnic groups: Portuguese 96.3%, other 3.7%
Religions: Roman Catholic 81%, other Christian 3.3%, other 0.6%, no religion 15.1%
Government type: Parliamentary democracy, with unicameral Assembly of the Republic; the president is the chief of state
Administration: 18 districts and 2 autonomous regions, divided into 308 municipalities
Economy: Led by services industries. Over the past decade, many firms run by the state have been privatised, and there have been many advances in the areas of finance and telecommunications. In 2011 high government debts and the collapse of two major banks led the country to borrow money from the International Monetary Fund and the EU in order to support its economy
GDP: $197.5 billion, made up of agriculture 2.4%, industry 23.1%, services 74.4%
Industries: Textiles, footwear, paper, rubber, plastic and metal products, chemicals, oil refining, fish canning, ceramics, electronics, transport and communications equipment, shipbuilding and refurbishment, wine, tourism
Labour force: 5.19 million
Unemployment: 12.2%
Currency: Euro
Calling code: +351
Language: Portuguese
Portugal in the EU: Joined 1986; 21 MEPs; the westernmost country in continental Europe
Portugal in the world: A founder member of NATO. A rich history of seafaring and discovery. An important colonial power, it lost a lot of its wealth and status after the devastating 1755 Lisbon earthquake and tsunami. In the 20th century, repressive governments ran Portugal, until a coup in 1974 ushered in democracy. This also led to independence for all Portugal's African colonies a year later

AUSTRIA

Capital: Vienna
Population: 8,662,588
Population growth rate: 0.01%
Median age: 44.3 years
Life expectancy at birth: 77.25 years for men, 83.2 years for women
Total land area: 83,870 sq km
Border countries: Czech Republic, Germany, Hungary, Italy, Liechtenstein, Slovakia, Slovenia, Switzerland
Coastline: 0 km (landlocked)
Ethnic groups: Austrian 81.1%, German 2.7%, Turk 2.2%, other 14%
Religions: Roman Catholic 73.6%, Protestant 4.7%, Muslim 4.2%, other or no religion 17.5%
Government type: Federal republic; president is chief of state; bicameral Federal Assembly consists of Federal Council and the National Council; when the 'Freedom Party' joined a coalition in 2000, its extreme far-right views caused alarm in the EU and led to some sanctions against Austria
Administration: Nine states divided into districts and municipalities
Economy: Modern market economy, relying a lot on its service industry. 47% of the land area is forested, so timber is a key product. Attractive to foreign investors due to its strategic location at the crossroads of Central Europe, close to the new EU economies
GDP: $385.5 billion, made up of agriculture 1.7%, industry 32.3%, services 65.8%
Industries: Construction, machinery, vehicles, food, metals, chemicals, lumber and wood processing, paper, communications equipment, tourism
Labour force: 4.43 million
Unemployment: 4.4%
Currency: Euro
Calling code: +43
Languages: German (official nationwide), Slovene (official in Carinthia), Croatian and Hungarian (official in Burgenland)
Austria in the EU: Joined in 1995; 18 MEPs
Austria in the world: Vienna is host to major international organisations, like the International Atomic Energy Agency; along with Switzerland, the only European country to declare itself 'permanently neutral'; under the Hapsburg dynasty, played a dominant role in Central Europe for centuries until 1918; has a rich cultural heritage and stunning mountain scenery

FINLAND

Capital: Helsinki
Population: 5,486,125
Population growth rate: 0.5%
Median age: 43.2 years
Life expectancy at birth: 77.2 years for men, 83.5 years for women
Total land area: 338,145 sq km
Border countries: Norway, Sweden, Russia
Coastline: 1,250 km (and has 187,888 lakes and 179,584 islands)
Ethnic groups: Finnish 89%, Swedish 5.3%, Russian 1.3%, other 4.4%
Religions: Protestant 75.3%, other 2.5%, no religion 22.1%
Government type: Republic; president is chief of state and there is a unicameral parliament
Administration: 19 regions divided into municipalities
Economy: A modern industrial state with a high level of income per person. Manufacturing sector is strong, and Finland exports many hi-tech electronics. There is also an advanced social welfare system
GDP: $221.54 billion, made up of agriculture 2.8%, industry 25.9%, services 71.2%
Industries: Metals, electronics, machinery and scientific instruments, shipbuilding, pulp and paper (two-thirds of Finland is covered in forest), foodstuffs, chemicals, textiles, clothing
Labour force: 2.38 million
Unemployment: 10.3%
Currency: Euro
Calling code: +358
Languages: Finnish, Swedish
Finland in the EU: Joined in 1995; 13 MEPs; the only Nordic EU state to adopt the euro
Finland in the world: Lived for centuries under Swedish rule, then under the shadow of the powerful Soviet Union for much of 20th century, even after independence in 1917. Famous for its 'White Nights' in the far north: for ten weeks in the summer, the Sun never sets (but also for eight weeks in winter the Sun never rises)

SWEDEN

Capital: Stockholm
Population: 9,845,155
Population growth rate: 0.93%
Median age: 41.2 years
Life expectancy at birth: 78.9 years for men, 83.6 years for women
Total land area: 449,964 sq km
Border countries: Finland and Norway
Coastline: 3,218 km
Ethnic groups: Swedish 79.9%, Finnish 2.4%, other 17.7%
Religions: Protestant 64.6%, other Christian 3%, Muslim 5%, other or no religion 27.4%
Government type: The Kingdom of Sweden is a constitutional monarchy; the monarch is the chief of state; there is a unicameral parliament
Administration: 20 county councils divided into 290 municipalities
Economy: Strong: a high standard of living based on mixing high-tech capitalism with big welfare benefits. Low unemployment
GDP: $552 billion, made up of agriculture 1.8%, industry 27.4%, services 70.8%
Industries: Iron and steel, precision equipment (bearings, radio and telephone parts, armaments), wood pulp and paper products, processed foods, motor vehicles
Labour force: 5.14 million
Unemployment: 6.2%
Currency: Swedish krone
Calling code: +46
Languages: Swedish; small Sami- and Finnish-speaking minorities
Sweden in the EU: Joined in 1995; 20 MEPs; Swedish voters said 'no' to adopting the euro in 2003
Sweden in the world: In the 17th and 18th centuries Sweden used warfare to expand its territory; it became a great power and grew to twice its present size. But the country went through the whole of the 20th century without any wars, taking a neutral stance. It is not a member of NATO. Many asylum seekers and refugees go to Sweden: over 10% of the population are immigrants

CYPRUS

Note: Cyprus has been divided between Greece and Turkey since 1974, when Turkish troops invaded the north. Cyprus is still divided after Greek Cypriots rejected a UN settlement in a referendum, while Turkish Cypriots approved it
Capital: Nicosia
Population: 1,141,168 (combined)
Population growth rate: 1.1%
Median age: 35.7 years
Life expectancy at birth: 77 years for men, 81.7 years for women
Total land area (Greek/Turkish areas combined): 9,250 sq km
Border countries: In the Mediterranean Sea, south of Turkey, the third-largest island (after Sicily and Sardinia)
Coastline: 648 km
Religions (Republic only): Orthodox 94.8%, other Christian 3.4%, Muslim 0.6%, other 1.2%
Ethnic groups (combined): Greek 77%, Turk 18%, other 5%
Government type: Republic. Greek Cypriots control the only internationally recognised government: the president is the head of state; it has a unicameral House of Representatives
Administration: Six districts
Economy: In the Republic of Cyprus, tourism and finance make up three-quarters of GDP. The Turkish Cypriot economy relies heavily on the Turkish government for support
GDP: $23.26 billion, made up of agriculture 2.4%, industry 10.6%, services 87.1%
Industries: Tourism, food and drink processing, cement and gypsum, ship repair, textiles
Industries: Tourism, food and drink processing, cement and gypsum, ship repair, textiles
Labour force: 356,700
Unemployment: 15.7%
Currency: Euro
Calling code: +357 or +90-392 in north
Languages: Greek, Turkish, English
Cyprus in the EU: Joined in 2004; 6 MEPs; the island was still divided when Cyprus became a member of the EU, so EU laws and benefits apply only to Greek Cypriots
Cyprus in the world: Known as the birthplace of Aphrodite, mythical Greek goddess of love; defined by enmity between Greek and Turkish Cypriots; was once a colony of Britain (independence agreed in 1960)

CZECH REPUBLIC

Capital: Prague
Population: 10,541,466
Population growth rate: 0.1%
Median age: 40.9 years
Life expectancy at birth: 75.2 years for men, 81.1 years for women
Total land area: 78,866 sq km
Border countries: Austria, Germany, Poland, Slovakia
Coastline: 0 km (landlocked)
Ethnic groups: Czech 64%, Moravian 5%, Slovak 1.4%, Polish 0.4%, other 26%
Religions: Roman Catholic 10.3%, Protestant 0.9%, other 9.4%, no religion 79.4%
Government type: Parliamentary democracy; the president is the chief of state; a bicameral parliament consists of the Senate and the Chamber of Deputies
Administration: Capital city, plus 13 regions
Economy: One of the most stable and prosperous of the post-Communist states of Central and Eastern Europe. Moves towards economic reform have been boosted by membership of the EU
GDP: $314.6 billion, made up of agriculture 1.8%, industry 39.6%, services 58.6%
Industries: Metals, machinery and equipment, motor vehicles, glass, armaments
Labour force: 5.3 million
Unemployment: 5.9%
Currency: Czech koruna
Calling code: +420
Language: Czech
The Czech Republic in the EU: Joined in 2004; 21 MEPs
The Czech Republic in the world: Rich cultural history and architectural treasures. As the nation of Czechoslovakia, it gained freedom from decades of Soviet rule in the peaceful 'Velvet Revolution' in 1989, before a 'Velvet Divorce' into two nations, the Czech Republic and Slovakia, in 1993. Joined NATO in 1999

ESTONIA

Capital: Tallinn
Population: 1,311,759
Population growth rate: –5.5%
Median age: 41.2 years
Life expectancy at birth: 71.7 years for men, 81.7 years for women
Total land area: 45,226 sq km
Border countries: Latvia and Russia
Coastline: 3,794 km
Ethnic groups: Estonian 69.7%, Russian 25.2%, Ukrainian 1.7%, Belarusian 0.9%, Finnish 0.6%, other 1.9%
Religions: Protestant 13.6%, Orthodox 12.8%, other 2.8%, no religion 70.8%
Government type: Parliamentary republic; the president is the chief of state; unicameral parliament; has experimented with Internet voting
Administration: 15 counties
Economy: One of the strongest economies of the new member states, making a smooth transition to a modern market economy; has strong links with the West, and has pegged its currency to the euro. Estonia is doing especially well in electronics and telecommunications. Forest covers 47% of the land
GDP: $20 billion, made up of agriculture 3.7%, industry 30.2%, services 66.1%
Industries: Engineering, electronics, wood and wood products, textiles, information technology, telecommunications
Labour force: 675,900
Unemployment: 7%
Currency: Euro
Calling code: +372
Languages: Estonian, Russian
Estonia in the EU: Joined in 2004; 6 MEPs
Estonia in the world: Gained independence in 1918, after centuries of Danish, Swedish, German and Russian rule. But the Soviet Union took control in 1940, and Estonia only got its freedom back in 1991, when communism collapsed. Joined NATO in 2004. The most northerly of the three former Soviet Baltic republics. The only country in the world where access to the Internet is a 'human right'

HUNGARY

Capital: Budapest
Population: 9,855,571
Population growth rate: –0.2%
Median age: 41.1 years
Life expectancy at birth: 70.9 years for men, 78.2 years for women
Total land area: 93,030 sq km
Border countries: Austria, Croatia, Romania, Serbia and Montenegro, Slovakia, Slovenia, Ukraine
Coastline: 0 km (landlocked)
Ethnic groups: Hungarian 78.2%, Roma 3.8%, German 16%, other 16.6%
Religions: Roman Catholic 38.9%, Protestant 13.8% Orthodox 0.1%, Jewish 0.1%, other 1.7%, no religion 45.3%
Government type: Parliamentary democracy; the president is chief of state and there is a unicameral National Assembly
Administration: Capital city plus 19 counties
Economy: Moved from a centrally planned to a market economy; a lot of foreign businesses own and invest in Hungarian firms. The private sector accounts for more than 80% of GDP
GDP: $241.5 billion, made up of agriculture 3.4%, industry 31.1%, services 65.5%
Industries: Mining, metals, construction materials, processed foods, textiles, chemicals, pharmaceuticals, motor vehicles
Labour force: 4.39 million
Unemployment: 6.8%
Currency: Hungarian forint
Calling code: +36
Language: Hungarian
Hungary in the EU: Joined in 2004; 21 MEPs
Hungary in the world: Member of NATO since 1999; strategically located on main land routes between Western Europe and Balkan Peninsula, and between Ukraine and Mediterranean basin; has largest lake in Europe, Lake Balaton; was under communist rule after the Second World War until the collapse of the Soviet Union: Hungary helped speed things up by opening its border with Austria so East Germans could escape to the west; a colourful mix of peoples: along with the majority Magyars, there are Roma, German, Slovak, Croat, Serb and Romanian minorities; amongst other things, Hungarians invented the match, the theory of the hydrogen bomb and the ballpoint pen

LATVIA

Capital: Riga
Population: 1,973,000
Population growth rate: –1%
Median age: 41.4 years
Life expectancy at birth: 69.5 years for men, 79 years for women
Total land area: 64,589 sq km
Border countries: Belarus, Estonia, Lithuania, Russia
Coastline: 531 km
Ethnic groups: Latvian 61.4%, Russian 26%, Belarusian 3.4%, Ukrainian 2.2%, Polish 1.3%, Lithuanian 1.2%, other 2.2%
Religions: Orthodox 31.3%, Roman Catholic 20%, Protestant 4.4%, other 10.6%, no religion 15.8%
Government type: Parliamentary democracy; the president is the chief of state, the prime minister is the head of the government and there is a unicameral parliament
Administration: 9 cities, 110 municipalities
Economy: The Latvian economy was badly hit by the 1998 Russian financial crisis. But since then it has changed its focus to deal with other EU countries, and growth rates have been high. Most companies, banks and real estate have been privatised, but some large enterprises are still in the hands of the state
GDP: $48.36 billion, made up of agriculture 4.4%, industry 26.3%, services 69.3%
Industries: Vehicles, synthetics, farm machinery, fertilisers, washing machines, radios, electronics, pharmaceuticals, processed foods, textiles
Labour force: 884,600
Unemployment: 9.1%
Currency: Euro
Calling code: +371
Languages: Latvian (official) 58.2%, Russian 37.5%, Lithuanian and other 4.3% (2000 census)
Latvia in the EU: Joined 2004; eight MEPs
Latvia in the world: Under foreign control from the 13th to the 20th centuries; brief spell of independence before Soviet rule in the 1940s, which finally ended in 1991; the middle of the three former Soviet Baltic republics; tensions with Russia over border issues; member of World Trade Organization, and joined NATO in 2004 shortly before membership of the EU – all impossible to imagine during the Soviet days

LITHUANIA

Capital: Vilnius
Population: 2,888,582
Population growth rate: –0.28%
Median age: 41.2 years
Life expectancy at birth: 70 years for men, 80.1 years for women
Total land area: 65,200 sq km
Border countries: Belarus, Latvia, Poland, Russia
Coastline: 99 km
Ethnic groups: Lithuanian 84%, Polish 6.6%, Russian 5.8%, Belarusian 1.2%, Ukrainian 0.5%, other 1.8%
Religions: Roman Catholic 77.2%, Orthodox 4.9%, Protestant 0.8%, other 0.9%, no religion 16.2%
Government type: Parliamentary democracy, unicameral parliament, president is head of state
Administration: Ten counties divided into 60 municipalities
Economy: Lithuania used to trade more with Russia than either of its Baltic state neighbours, but after the Russian financial crisis in 1998 it was forced to turn more to the West. It was given membership of the World Trade Organization in 2001, and growth rates in recent years have been high, although a lot of people in the country are still poor
GDP: $40.7 billion, made up of agriculture 3.5%, industry 23.6%, services 65.5%
Industries: Metal-cutting machine tools, electric motors, television sets, refrigerators and freezers, petroleum refining, shipbuilding (small ships), furniture making, textiles, food processing, fertilisers, agricultural machinery, optical equipment, electronic components, computers, amber
Labour force: 1.47 million
Unemployment: 8.3%
Currency: Euro
Calling code: +370
Languages: Lithuanian (official) 82%, Russian 8%, Polish 5.6%, other and unspecified 4.4% also spoken (2001 census)
Lithuania in the EU: Joined 2004; 11 MEPs
Lithuania in the world: Lithuania helped to hasten the end of Soviet rule with its 'Singing Revolution'; it became the first of the Soviet republics to declare its independence in 1990, after fifty years of rule by Moscow. The last Russian troops withdrew in 1993. Lithuania joined NATO in spring 2004

MALTA

Capital: Valletta
Population: 445,426
Population growth rate: 0.9%
Median age: 40.9 years
Life expectancy at birth: 79.1 years for men, 82.2 years for women
Total land area: 316 sq km
Border countries: Archipelago with three main inhabited islands in the Mediterranean
Coastline: 196.8 km
Ethnic groups: Maltese 95.2%, other 4.8%
Religions: Roman Catholic 98%, other 2%
Government type: Republic; unicameral House of Representatives; president is chief of state
Administration: 5 regions divided into 68 local councils
Economy: Malta's main source of income is tourism: because of tourist arrivals, the population temporarily triples every year. It has an attractive geographic location and a hard-working labour force. The economy also depends on foreign trade and manufacturing
GDP: $11.22 billion, made up of agriculture 1.4%, industry 25.3%, services 73.3%
Industries: Tourism, electronics, shipbuilding and repair, construction, food and beverages, textiles, footwear, clothing, tobacco
Labour force: 190,400
Unemployment: 5.9%
Currency: Euro
Calling code: +356
Languages: Maltese, English
Malta in the EU: Joined 2004, the smallest of the ten new countries welcomed into the club; 6 MEPs
Malta in the world: A history of colonial rule going back centuries: Phoenicians, Greeks, Romans, Arabs, the French and the British have all colonised Malta

POLAND

Capital: Warsaw
Population: 38,483,957
Population growth rate: 0%
Median age: 39.5 years
Life expectancy at birth: 72.3 years for men, 80.4 years for women
Total land area: 312,685 sq km
Border countries: Belarus, Czech Republic, Germany, Lithuania, Russia, Slovakia, Ukraine
Coastline: 491 km
Ethnic groups: Polish 97.7%, other European 0.9%, other 1.4%
Religions: Roman Catholic 87.5%, Orthodox 0.7%, other 1%, no religion 10.8%
Government type: Democratic republic; Council of Ministers led by prime minister; parliament with upper and lower house; president is head of state, chosen by popular vote
Administration: 16 provinces, divided into 379 counties
Economy: Poland has made significant market reforms: many state-owned companies are now run by private businesses. Unemployment is the highest in the EU, with widespread poverty in rural areas. Agriculture is very important: 16% of the population work in farming. Many farms are small and inefficient, but Poland is benefiting from billions of euros in EU funds, and farmers have begun to gain through higher food prices and subsidies
GDP: $1 trillion, made up of agriculture 3.5%, industry 34.2%, services 62.3%
Industries: Machine building, iron and steel, coal mining, chemicals, shipbuilding, food processing, glass, beverages, textiles
Labour force: 17.92 million
Unemployment: 9.7%
Currency: Polish zloty
Calling code: +48
Language: Polish
Poland in the EU: Joined 2004; 51 MEPs; a key location at one of the EU's external borders
Poland in the world: At the centre of Europe; has a thousand-year history: sometimes independent, sometimes dominated by others; several million people, half of them Jews, died in the Second World War. Poland was a key player in the first moves away from communist rule in the 1980s; joined NATO in 1999; raised its profile internationally when it sent Polish troops to support the US-led invasion of Iraq

SLOVAKIA

Capital: Bratislava
Population: 5,415,949
Population growth rate: 0.1%
Median age: 39.2 years
Life expectancy at birth: 72.1 years for men, 80.1 years for women
Total land area: 49,033 sq km
Border countries: Austria, Czech Republic, Hungary, Poland, Ukraine
Coastline: 0 km (landlocked)
Ethnic groups: Slovak 80.7%, Hungarian 8.5%, Roma 2%, other 8.8%
Religions: Roman Catholic 62%, Protestant 8.9%, other Christian 4.7%, other 0.8%, no religion 23.6%
Government type: Parliamentary democracy with a unicameral National Council of the Slovak Republic
Administration: Eight regions divided into 79 districts
Economy: Slovakia is a popular place for foreign investors. For example, most banks are now in foreign hands. Many reforms have been made and economic growth has been strong, though unemployment is still a worry
GDP: $132.4 billion, made up of agriculture 3.8%, industry 36.4%, services 59.8%
Industries: Metals, food and beverages, electricity, gas, coke, oil, nuclear fuel, chemicals and manmade fibres, machinery, paper and printing, earthenware and ceramics, transport vehicles, textiles, electrical and optical apparatus, rubber products
Labour force: 2.72 million
Unemployment: 12.2%
Currency: Euro
Calling code: +421
Languages: Slovak; about 10% of population speak Hungarian
Slovakia in the EU: Joined in 2004; 13 MEPs
Slovakia in the world: At the heart of Europe, with a history closely linked to its neighbours, but proud of its own distinct language and culture; was part of Czechoslovakia until the 'Velvet Divorce' in 1993, when the two countries agreed to split; member of NATO since 2004

SLOVENIA

Capital: Ljubljana
Population: 2,063,077
Population growth rate: 0.2%
Median age: 42.8 years
Life expectancy at birth: 77.2 years for men, 83.6 years for women
Total land area: 20,273 sq km
Border countries: Austria, Croatia, Hungary, Italy
Coastline: 46.6 km
Ethnic groups: Slovene 83.1%, Serb 2%, Croat 1.8%, Bosniak 1.1%, others 12%
Religions: Roman Catholic 57.8%, Eastern Orthodox 2.3%, other Christian 0.8%, Muslim 2.4%, other or no religion 36.7%
Government type: Parliamentary democratic republic: a bicameral parliament consisting of a National Assembly and National Council
Administration: 200 municipalities and 11 urban municipalities
Economy: Slovenia was always one of the most prosperous regions of the former Yugoslavia, and people have a better income per head than in any of the other EU countries that joined in 2004. However foreign investment has been low and the country was severely hurt by the economic downturn after 2008
GDP: $49,506 billion, made up of agriculture 2.5%, industry 36.9%, services 60.6%
Industries: Iron, steel and aluminium products, lead and zinc smelting, electronics (including military electronics), trucks, electric power equipment, wood products, textiles, chemicals, machine tools
Labour force: 926,000
Unemployment: 9.4%
Currency: Euro
Calling code: +386
Languages: Slovene Hungarian, Italian, Croat, Serb
Slovenia in the EU: Joined in 2004; 8 MEPs, the only former Yugoslav republic to be in the first wave of candidates for membership
Slovenia in the world: Spectacular mountains and thick forests; gained independence from Yugoslavia after a 10-day war in 1991; member of NATO

BULGARIA

Capital: Sofia
Population: 7,364,570
Population growth rate: −0.52%
Median age: 40 years
Life expectancy at birth: 70.6 for men, 77.6 for women
Total land area: 110,994 sq km
Border countries: Greece, Macedonia, Serbia, Romania, Turkey
Coastline: 354 km
Ethnic groups: Bulgarian 84.8%, Turk 8.8%, Roma 4.9%, other 1.5%
Religions: Eastern Orthodox 59.4%, other Christian 1.6%, Muslim 7.9%, none 31.1%
Government type: Parliamentary democratic republic with a single-chamber parliament; the directly elected president is largely a figurehead
Administration: 27 provinces and the metropolitan capital province, divided into 264 municipalities
Economy: Strong industrialised economy that has grown fast in recent years and has attracted considerable foreign investment
GDP: $128.1 billion, made up of agriculture 8.6%, industry 27.3%, services 64.1%
Industries: Energy, mining, metallurgy, machinery, agriculture, tourism
Labour force: 3.53 million
Unemployment: 8.3%
Currency: Bulgarian lev
Calling code: +359
Languages: Bulgarian, Turkish, Roma
Bulgaria in the EU: An EU member since 2007 with 17 MEPs, Bulgaria enjoys good relations with its neighbours with close ties to both Romania and Greece
Bulgaria in the world: In south-eastern Europe, bordering the Black Sea. It was part of the Ottoman Empire for 500 years, and a one-party communist state for nearly half a century after the Second World War. A NATO member since 2004

ROMANIA

Capital: Bucharest
Population: 19,511,000
Population growth rate: 0.22%
Median age: 39.8 years
Life expectancy at birth: 68.7 for men, 75.9 for women
Total land area: 238,391 sq km
Border countries: Bulgaria, Serbia, Hungary, Ukraine, Moldova
Coastline: 245 km
Ethnic groups: Romanian 88.9%, Hungarian 6.5%, Romani 3.3%, other 0.4%
Religions: Eastern Orthodox 86.5%, Protestant 6.9%, Roman Catholic 4.6%, other 2%
Government type: Multi-party republic in which the president and government share executive functions
Administration: 42 prefectures
Economy: Developing economy with high growth rates, its capital city is one of the largest financial and industrial centres in eastern Europe
GDP: $199.04 billion, made up of services 52.2%, industry 35.7%, agriculture 12.1%
Industries: Electrical machinery, textiles, construction materials, metallurgy, chemicals, food processing, oil refining
Labour force: 9.24 million
Unemployment: 6.8%
Currency: Romania leu
Calling code: +40
Languages: Romanian, Hungarian, Romani
Romania in the EU: Joined the EU in 2007 and actively supports the admission of former Soviet republics in eastern Europe and the Caucasus to the Union; because of its large Hungarian minority, Romania has strong relations with Hungary. Has 32 MEPs
Romania in the world: A member of NATO since 2004, Romania has close relations with Moldova, once a province of the country

CROATIA

Capital: Zagreb
Population: 4,284,889
Population growth rate: −0.3%
Median age: 42.1 years
Life expectancy at birth: 72.8 for men, 80.2 years for women
Total land area: 56,594 sq km
Border countries: Slovenia, Hungary, Serbia, Bosnia-Herzegovina, Montenegro
Coastline: 5,835 km
Ethnic groups: Croats 90.4%, Serbs 4.4%, others 5.2%
Religions: Roman Catholic 86.3%, Eastern Orthodox 4.4%, Muslim 1.5%, other 7.8%
Government type: Parliamentary democracy with a single chamber and a directly elected president
Administration: 21 counties, subdivided into 127 cities and 429 municipalities
Economy: Dominated by services, notably tourism
GDP: $57.156 billion, made up agriculture 4.5%, industry 26.6%, services 68.9%
Industries: Shipbuilding, food processing, chemicals, tourism
Labour force: 1,677,819
Unemployment: 17.9%
Currency: Croatian kuna
Calling code: +385
Languages: Croatian, Serbian
Croatia in the EU: The newest member of the EU joined in 2013, having previously resolved its maritime border with Slovenia. Has 11 MEPs
Croatia in the world: In 1991 Croatia declared its independence from Yugoslavia and fought a four-year war against Serbian forces. Croatia has been a member of NATO since 2009 and seeks to enhance its relations with its neighbours

WAITING IN THE WINGS

Six more countries are hoping to join the European Union soon.

ALBANIA

Applied for membership in 2009, recognized as an official candidate in 2014

Capital: Tirana

Population: 2,893,005

Total land area: 165,048 sq km

Economy: Rich in natural resources, Albania relies on agriculture, food processing, cement, mining and tourism

GDP: $32,259 billion, made up of agriculture 18.4%, industry 16.3%, services 65.3%

Official language: Albanian

Currency: Albanian lek

Defence: Member of NATO since 2009

MACEDONIA

Applied for membership in 2005 but has yet to start formal negotiations; its candidature has been held up as Greece objects to it calling itself the Republic of Macedonia, as Macedonia is also the name of a Greek region

Capital: Skopje

Population: 2,069,162

Total land area: 25,713 sq km

Economy: The poorest republic of former Yugoslavia, Macedonia meets its own food needs but relies on imports of fuel and machinery; heavily reliant on remittances from overseas workers and on foreign aid

GDP: $12 billion, made up of agriculture 8.8%, industry 21.3%, services 69.8%

Official language: Macedonian

Currency: Macedonian denar

Defence: Expected to join NATO in 2016

ICELAND

Applied for membership in 2009 but suspended its application in 2013 pending a referendum on membership

Capital: Reykjavik

Population: 329,100

Total land area: 102,775 sq km

Economy: Iceland has a mixed economy powered by abundant hydroelectric and geothermal power sources

GDP: $16.7 billion, made up of agriculture 6%, industry 22.4%, services 71.7%

Official language: Icelandic

Currency: Icelandic korna

Defence: Member of NATO since 1949, although the country has no standing army

MONTENEGRO

Applied for membership in 2008, recognised as an official candidate in 2010

Capital: Podgorica

Population: 629,029

Total land area: 13,812 sq km

Economy: A mainly service-based economy with an important tourist sector; exports aluminium and other metals

GDP: $7.4 billion, made up of agriculture 6.3%, industry 20.9%, services 72.8%

Official language: Montenegrin

Currency: Euro

Defence: Expected to join NATO in 2016

SOME EU ACHIEVEMENTS

- There is now a single market that makes it easier for EU nations to buy and sell goods and services to each other.
- The euro is used by 19 nations and has the highest value of coins and banknotes in circulation of any currency in the world
- The EU has one of the most powerful economies in the world, and gives more money than anyone else to help developing countries
- EU citizens are free to live, work, vote and retire in the country of their choice

Two other countries are potential candidates:

SERBIA

Applied for membership in 2009, recognised as an official candidate in 2012

Capital: Belgrade

Population: 7,041,599

Total land area: 77,474 sq km

Economy: Serbia has received much inward investment in car plants, food processing and other industries; its biggest trading partner is the EU

GDP: $95,492 billion, made up of agriculture 8.2%, industry 36.9%, services 54.9%

Official language: Serbian

Currency: Serbian dinar

Defence: Works with NATO but not a member and shows no sign of joining

BOSNIA-HERZEGOVINA

Applied for membership in 2016, but still affected by its brutal civil war of 1992–95

Capital: Sarajevo

Population: 3,871,643

Total land area: 51,197 sq km

Economy: Still harmed by the civil war, Bosnia-Herzegovina has a highly skilled workforce and strength in metals, agriculture, and other industries

GDP: $15,568 billion, made up of agriculture 8.1%, industry 28.4%, services 65.3%

Official languages: Bosnian, Croatian, Serbian

Currency: Convertible mark (the currency was formerly aligned with the German mark) which is pegged to the euro

Defence: Linked with NATO since 2010 and is soon expected to join the alliance

TURKEY

Applied for membership in 1987, recognised as an official candidate in 1999, but talks have since stalled following objections from other EU members against its proposed membership and poor record on human rights

Capital: Ankara

Population: 78,741,053

Total land area: 783,562 sq km

Economy: The 17th largest economy in the world, Turkey is a major car producer and ship builder, as well as a producer of textiles and agricultural products

GDP: $1,641 trillion, made up of agriculture 8.9%, industry 27.3%, services 63.8%

Official language: Turkish

Currency: Turkish lira

Defence: Member of NATO since 1952

KOSOVO

Hopes to join the EU, but five member states have yet to recognise its independence. The country has yet to join the UN and 85 of its members do not recognise its independence

Capital: Pristina

Population: 1,859,203

Total land area: 10.908 sq km

Economy: One of the poorest areas in Europe with around half the population under the official poverty line

GDP: $16.93 billion, made up of agriculture 12.9%, industry 22.6%, services 64.5%

Official languages: Albanian, Serbian

Currency: Euro

Defence: Aims to join NATO in the future

- The EU has kept the peace between its members for more than 60 years and now dominates the European continent
- Through EU programmes like Erasmus, some two million young people have studied in another European country

- The Union helps its poorer regions by giving money for things like transport projects, and training people to give them new skills
- Because of laws on the environment, Europe's rivers and beaches are among the cleanest in the world

EU SUMMARY

Location: Europe, between Belarus, Ukraine, Russia, southeastern Europe and the North Atlantic Ocean

Capital: Brussels, Belgium. The Council of the EU meets in Brussels, the Parliament in Strasbourg, France, and the Court of Justice in Luxembourg

Population: 508,191,116

Population growth rate: 2.2%

Fertility rate: 1.58 children born for every woman in the EU

Age distribution: 0–14 years: 15.4%; 15–24 years: 11.2%; 25–54 years: 42.1%; 55–64 years: 12.7%; 65 and over: 18.5%

Life expectancy at birth: 75.7 for men, 82.1 for women

Net migration: 3.3 migrants per 1,000

Total land area: 4,324,782 sq km

Border countries: Albania, Andorra, Belarus, Bosnia-Herzegovina, Holy See, Liechtenstein, Macedonia, Moldova, Monaco, Montenegro, Norway, Russia, San Marino, Serbia, Switzerland, Turkey, Ukraine

Lowest/highest point: Lammefjord, Denmark -7 m; Zuidplaspolder, Netherlands -7 m/Mont Blanc, France 4,807 m

Coastline: 65,993 km

Natural hazards: From flooding in coastal areas, to avalanches in mountains; from volcanoes in Italy to earthquakes in the south; from droughts in southern Europe to ice floes in the Baltic

Religions: Roman Catholic 48%, Protestant 12%, Orthodox 8%, other Christian 4%, Muslim 2%, other 3%, no belief 23%

Government type: A hybrid intergovernmental organisation.

European Commission: Member governments decide who will be the president of the Commission; the president-delegate appoints the other 27 members, one nominated from each member state; European Parliament confirms the whole Commission for a five-year term

European Council: The main decision-making body; chaired by its own president, it brings together heads of state and government and the President of the Commission at least twice a year to push for progress on major EU issues

European Parliament: 751 seats split among member states according to their population. EU voters (18 and over) choose members of parliament for five-year term

Economy: The EU tries to reach agreement between 28 nations on all economic issues, but member states do not always agree. There is a big range of average yearly income. Twelve EU member states adopted the euro as their common currency on 1 January 1999. Britain, Sweden and Denmark did not. Since then, another seven new member nations have adopted the euro, with others to follow.

GDP: $18,399 trillion, made up of agriculture 2.1%, industry 27.3%, services 70.5%

Industries: Among the world's largest and most technologically advanced, the European Union industrial base includes: metal production and processing, metal products, petroleum, coal, cement, chemicals, pharmaceuticals, aerospace, rail transportation equipment, passenger and commercial vehicles, construction equipment, industrial equipment, shipbuilding, electrical power equipment, machine tools and automated manufacturing systems, electronics and telecommunications equipment, fishing, food and beverage processing, furniture, paper, textiles, tourism in services

Unemployment: 9.3%

Exports: $3,182 trillion, mainly to the USA 16.5%, Switzerland 9.7% and China 8.5%

Imports: $2,902 trillion, mainly from China 16.6%, Russia 11.6% and the USA 11.8%

Currencies: Euro, British pound, Bulgarian lev, Croatian kuna, Czech koruna, Danish krone, Hungarian forint, Polish zloty, Romanian leu, Swedish krona

Official languages: 24: Bulgarian, Croatian, Czech, Danish, Dutch, English, Estonian, Finnish, French, German, Greek, Hungarian, Italian, Irish, Latvian, Lithuanian, Maltese, Polish, Portuguese, Romania, Slovak, Slovene, Spanish, Swedish

EU in the world: The EU has its own flag, anthem, founding date and currency

Accession   Signing up to become a member

Asylum   The chance for people to live safely in a new country, if it is dangerous for them to live in their own

Audit   A close examination of how an organisation is run, and whether it is sticking to the rules

Co-decision   Making a decision by reaching agreement with each other

Democracy   A system where the people can choose who runs their country

Development aid   Money that is given to people who need help, especially in poorer countries

Discrimination   Unfair treatment

Diversity   Variety

Duties   A government tax, particularly on imports

Economy   The money and resources of a country, and how the government looks after them

EU constitution   A set of guidelines and rules on the way the EU should be run

EU enlargement   Making the EU club bigger by allowing new members to join.

EU treaty   Agreements made between member states of the EU

Eurosceptic   A person who is opposed to increasing the powers of the EU

Federation   A system of government where states are united but decide some things for themselves

Free trade   Buying and selling without rules giving an unfair advantage to one side or the other

GDP or **Gross Domestic Product**   The value of everything that a country produces in one year

GNI or **Gross National Income**   The total domestic product and foreign income earned by a country each year

Immigration   Coming into a foreign country to live there

Institution   An organisation with its own rules and customs

Monetary policy   Agreements on how to handle money matters

Parliament   A place where politicians meet to decide the laws of the country

Peacekeeping missions   Troops sent to a country to maintain peace after conflict

Prosperity   Wealth

Referendum   The chance for people to vote on an important issue

Reunified   Countries joining together again after they have been split up

Single market   A trading area with no barriers to the free movement of money, people and goods

Sovereignty   The authority of a state to govern itself with supreme power over its affairs

Subsidies   Money given to try to fix prices at a certain level

Taxation   Rules on how much money people and businesses must pay to the state, depending on how much they earn

The United Nations   An international organisation that tries to push for peace between different countries

WEBSITES

http://europa.eu

Gateway to the official European Union website

www.europarl.eu/news/public/default_en.htm

Official European Parliament website

ec.europa.eu

Official EU Commission website

www.consilium.europa.eu/en/european-council

Official EU Council website

www.cia.gov/library/publications/resources/the-world-factbook/index.html

CIA World Factbook: guides available to each EU country, and the EU itself

www.encyclopedia.com/topic/European_Union.aspx

Facts, pictures and information about the European Union

http://www.theguardian.com/world/europe-news

Useful EU resource for older readers

INDEX